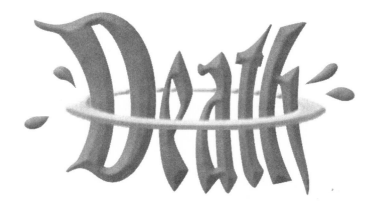

Is A Relative
Thing

Holly Patrone
http://www.hpatrone.com
info@hpatrone.com
cell:631.559.9259

Quantity discounts are available on bulk orders. Contact sales@TAGPublishers.com for more information.

TAG Publishing, LLC
2618 S. Lipscomb
Amarillo, TX 79109
www.TAGPublishers.com
Office (806) 373-0114
Fax (806) 373-4004
info@TAGPublishers.com

ISBN: 978-1-934606-08-7

First Edition

Copyright © 2011 Holly Patrone

Is A Relative
Thing

Holly Patrone

About the Author

Photo by Vladimir Ratikan

International prizewinning author, Holly Patrone, won her first fiction award in the fourth grade. She lives on the eastern end of Long Island with her husband, the two youngest of her five children and three Boston Terriers. Holly's convinced the dogs love her best because they jump up and down for ten minutes when she comes home. Everyone else just wants dinner. She eats dark chocolate and shrimp though usually not at the same time. Mostly she writes.

Please feel free to visit http://www.hpatrone.com/

Dedication

For Joe, Rob, Josh, Nick and Marisa. Of them, I couldn't be more proud.

Chapter 1

"I take a very practical view of raising children. I put a sign in each of their rooms: 'Checkout time is eighteen years.'"
                                                    – Erma Bombeck

Some days I feel like a breast stuck in a mammography machine. I'm held in place by forces I can't control, squashed by my life, with no way to break free of the grip. Man, the person who said life was like a box of chocolates didn't know how good he had it.

At least with chocolate, you get to taste and switch. I took a moment to mull over whether that strategy would work with the job and the kids and shook away the thought, entertaining though it was. The way I figure it, I would end up tasting an awful lot of chocolate and there would just be more of me to stuff into the next mammogram.

Death Is A Relative Thing

My name is April Serao. I'm of Italian-American heritage. My family is big. Holiday dinners look and sound like fights to anyone not Italian, and every uncle, nephew or male cousin I have is named Sammy. I work as a Technical Support Engineer for a tiny computer company called Tin Cup Software, TCS for short. I get to listen to people's problems all day long and try to fix them. The problems, not the people. It's a lot like being a wife and mother, but I get paid for it.

My husband Sal died six years ago while engaged in sex, which, as an aside, was part of my fortieth birthday present. The good news is that he was having sex with me, we both managed to finish the job before he checked out, and I didn't have to fight for custody of the kids. The bad news? Well, besides the fact that he was no help around the house, we got along well and truly liked each other, which is more than you can say for most married people. It took a long time for me and the boys to work through his death, but we've done ok.

Of course, people do talk and word got around about how Sal met his unfortunate demise, so dating has been on the slow side. Actually, it's been nonexistent. Men make sure they put physical distance between me and them as if WHAM! they'll have an orgasm right on the spot and keel over if they are within five feet of me.

Occasionally, though, it does work to my advantage—like the time Rich down at Chuck's butcher shop was weighing my shank steak with his finger on the scale. I leaned in as close as I could, draped my body across the counter and, in my best sultry voice, said, "Hun, you're not giving me enough meat." He turned a ghastly shade of grey, hastily threw another two pounds (give or take) on the scale, and barely took the time to wrap it up before he pushed it at me. I heard the guy checked his vital signs for an hour. Next time I need to try that with filet mignon.

Anyway, it had been a long day at work and all I wanted was to get home, which unfortunately meant I had to drive by Mrs. Krupshaw's house. Helen Krupshaw is old by any standard and lives two doors down from me in a meticulously kept white and red ranch. She sits on her front porch in a big blue rocking chair whenever the weather permits and gives me the finger as I drive by. She probably can't remember what she ate for lunch, but she does recall that eleven years ago she caught my oldest son Chris playing kamikaze helicopter with her TV antenna. Anyway, every time she sees me, she flips me the bird. Tonight was no exception. I smiled and waved.

I pulled my car into the concrete driveway, turned it off, yanked up the handbrake and took a deep breath. I never want to leave my car. It's a chili pepper red Mini Cooper S. It's clean, mine, and too small to hold my kids. My car is my sanity—the insulating bubble that, barring the Mrs. Krupshaw drive-by, keeps me safe and happy. My house, on the other hand, looks like the inside of a bag lady's purse.

Home is a very modest traditional blue cape in a very modest neighborhood on not-so-modest Long Island. Too far east to be affluent and too far west to be trendy, it sits squarely between Shoram, which features a defunct nuclear plant, and Brookhaven National Laboratory, which purports to have a nuclear something or another.

I don't worry too much about paying my electric bill. I figure if they ever turn me off, I'll just read by a few radioactive isotopes.

As I walked up to the door my mind barely registered the bikes piled on the front porch along with a few faded deck chairs, an assortment of dead potted plants, and numerous multicolored paintball splats on the blue siding. Sometimes I do notice how bad it is, but only during PMS week. That's when I start to bark out cleaning orders. My kids have learned not to pay attention to any threats of castration during those few days each month. Like Pavlov's dogs, they're conditioned; they know that if they buy me dark chocolate and ride out the storm, the porch can stay that way until the house is condemned and they'll never have to move a thing.

The door swung open and Brian, my 15-year-old, appeared. He's the youngest of my three sons.

"What's for dinner?"

Brian stands about 5'8 with dark wavy hair that he keeps it on the long side. He has serious eyes and killer verbal skills.

Every sentence he utters has exactly three words. Never one word, never twenty. Always three. I am not sure what to make of it, but the school psychologist hasn't called me yet, so I figure he's ok.

"Well, hello! Nice to see you too," I said. "Don't know—haven't thought about dinner yet. What do you want?"

"How 'bout pizza?"

"You buying, kiddo?"

"Okay, chicken then. Just cook fast." He leaned against the refrigerator and held his stomach in mock anguish.

I am the queen of the twenty-minute dinner. If it can't be on the table within that time, it's not on the menu. I took some chicken strips from the freezer and started frying them in a pan. In deference to their frozen state, I turned the burner on high.

The clock on the stove said 6:59 p.m. when the phone rang. I was tired but knew that if I ignored the call, she'd be on my doorstep with an EMT and a first aid kit within seven minutes. I snatched up the phone on the first ring.

"Hey, Mom," I said, without checking caller i.d. Ever since my husband died, Marie Stallone, my mother and the extended-family matriarch, has called at precisely 7:00 p.m. every night. Rain, sleet, snow, gall bladder operation—nothing keeps her from that phone. Big Ben sets time by her.

"There's a great sale on eggs at the Quick Mart—two for one—and milk is on sale at Shop-Rite. I got to the early bird sale at Stonards at 6:00 a.m. and can you believe they had sold out their tomato seedlings already?"

I can only listen to my mother on the phone for about a minute before she starts sounding like the adults on a Charlie Brown cartoon and my mind wanders.

Occasionally she does refocus my attention with a carefully placed word. Chocolate, coffee, money, and the phrase "I'm sending you all to Disneyworld" will usually ensure that I'm listening. None of them came up this time, so my mind drifted. Looking through the stack of mail on the counter I started sorting. Bills go into piles such as "ignore for another month," "pay when I hit the lottery," and "ignore even if I hit the lottery, just on principle." Advertisements get filed under "I wouldn't buy even if I had the money" (I store *this* pile in the recycling bin) and "buy after I hit the lottery." The rest of the mail now rested in my hands.

The Magazine Publishers Sweepstakes promised me yet again that I may already be a winner. Every Super Bowl Sunday for the last seven years, I've dressed up, taken off my fuzzy slippers, cleaned the front hallway with a vengeance, and waited for the Prize Patrol to grace my doorstep with a load of balloons and a very large check. They never show, but I still find myself compelled to open the envelope and order two magazines. I stowed the letter under the bills so the kids didn't see and laugh at me. I still refuse to throw it away "just in case." I'm terrified of being the person who tosses the winning numbers. I've looked on the Internet to see if there's some twelve-step program to cure me of this obsession, to no avail.

Somewhere in the back of my brain, I realized that my mother was still talking. Tuesday, tickets, father won't go....none of my happy buzzwords yet. She was asking me a question, so I managed to fake a sincere, "Uh-huh, sure," and tried to catch up with the conversation.

"So?" she asked. "You'll come with me?"

"Sure, mom. No problem...when? Tomorrow night? Ok."

"Great! I am so excited! I hope we get to speak with Sal."

Sal? Oh, boy, what did I miss? "Ma...Sal is dead, been that way for a long time. I'm not sure he is going to be holding up his end of the conversation."

"But that's what this guy does! He talks to the dead! Remember? He was on cable! I'll pick you up at seven!"

Groan. I have to learn to listen at least a little when she speaks.

"Mom, maybe you should make it 7:30. You wouldn't want to miss calling me, would you?"

Fortunately, I had to cut the call short to deal with the smoke alarm going off. Damn! The chicken!

I raced to the stove, pulled the smoldering pan off the burner, and tossed it onto a breadboard. I grabbed a towel and fanned it madly at the smoke alarm trying to shut off the noise. I heard one of the boys yell, "Dinner's ready!" and the three of them thundered down the stairs into the kitchen.

Smartasses, all of them. They got that from their father.

After dinner when I start to clean off the table, that's the boys' cue to scatter. Scott and Brian left quickly, probably headed to another county. When Chris picked up a few glasses and put them in the sink, my mom radar went into overdrive.

"Ok, what's wrong?" I asked.

"What makes you think something's wrong?"

"You're clearing the table. You have never shown any interest or natural talent in that skill set. Why start now?"

He laughed in a way that warmed my heart and tossed me a quick smile.

He's the oldest of the boys, quick to laugh and, in some ways, very grown up since his dad died. He's a talented musician on a number of different instruments. Much to the neighbor's delight he prefers the electric guitar attached to a refrigerator-sized amp. He's good looking and girls have been known to stop him in the mall and press their phone numbers into his palm.

"Mom…how did you know dad was the person you wanted to marry?"

Oh boy. I didn't know that I wanted to marry him but the proverbial rabbit died and it seemed like the right thing to do. However, I wasn't sure I should pass on that particular nugget of wisdom to my child.

"Well, hun, your dad kind of grew on me. We just assumed one day that we would get married. It felt right." Besides, I was seven months pregnant.

"Mom. I think I'm in love."

"Hmmm…with who? The girl with the long bleached-blonde hair who totally disappears when she turns sideways? What was her name…"

"No, mom, not her."

"The short-brown haired girl with the size D cups and the belly piercing?"

"Nope."

"Aha! It has to be Amy then, right? Curly blonde hair, belly piercing and thong?"

"Yeah, but—hey, how did you know about the thong?"

H-m-m-m-m-m.

"Let me ask you kiddo, do you get excited whenever she walks into a room?"

"Oh, yeah." His eyes lit up and his mouth turned into a grin.

"Do you always want to be with her?"

"Oh, yeah!"

"Does it feel good when your friends see you with her?"

"Well, yeah, ma."

"Chris, do you hold her head when she's throwing up? Go to the mall with her when she's shopping for shoes? Do you like being with her when she is babysitting, or when you both have no money? Could you picture her going grey, forty pounds heavier, twenty years older, with stretch marks? How about with a baby on each hip?"

"Ohhhhhh, MAAAAA!"

"Listen Chris," I said. "Go take a cold shower. Wait about two years and then talk to me about it. In the meantime, make sure you guys are well protected."

He left quickly, as he often does after these heartwarming mother-son discussions. As usual, I finished the kitchen cleanup solo.

Death Is A Relative Thing

Chapter 2

"No man goes before his time, unless the boss leaves early."

— Groucho Marx

The next morning after hitting the snooze alarm for 45 minutes, I bolted out of bed, late again. I started coffee and checked on the boys. They were gone. Chris works as a barista for Espresso House, where he sells overpriced coffee and scones to early-morning commuters rushing to the city, so he heads out early each day. I was fairly confident that Scott and Brian had gone to school, although occasionally they play billiards downtown and conveniently forget about getting on the bus.

I managed my way through a shower, then towel-dried my hair and threw in some gel. I dressed quickly in a light blue knit sweater, jeans that were dark enough to promise thinning qualities and my favorite low leather clogs. I grabbed my laptop, keys, purse and travel mug, then headed to my car.

Mini Coopers have teeny tiny cup holders that accommodate travel mugs roughly the size of thimbles so I had to place the coffee between my legs. This, by the way, is not such a bad way to start the day when your husband has been dead for six years. I rooted through my purse for makeup while backing out of the driveway. Over the past decade I've perfected the art of simultaneously driving a stick shift, applying blush, drinking coffee, talking on a cell phone, and getting from point A to point B in one piece. There are times it can get challenging, as when I'm driving on the Long Island Expressway in rush-hour traffic, because shifting takes priority and sometimes my mascara goes in my ear, but I have been doing this for years and can still hear, so I continue to press my luck.

I pulled into the TCS parking lot. TCS is housed in one half of a small grey industrial building with a 70s flavor to it—asymmetrical, severe and dated. Otherwise it's as nondescript as any of the hundreds of other industrial buildings that surround it. The front window angles in, defying gravity. I parked my car as close to the building as I could get and power-walked to the front door.

"Well, how nice of you to join us, Sunshine!" said Carl, the hottest receptionist this side of the Nassau county line. He's not tall but well built with dark skin, long black hair tied at the nape of his neck, and eyes so green they startle. He dresses in chinos and silk button-down shirts that coordinate well with his workstation, a large contemporary metal and wood desk just to the left of the front door. From there he handles the phones, takes delivery of lunchtime pizzas, and emails his boyfriend. Sigh. He greets each employee personally every day and is our living, breathing time clock.

"Hey, Carl. Yeah, wow, horrible traffic today. Can't believe I got here so late."

"Sure thing, Sunshine." I was graced with a side-swept smile and a wink as he buzzed me through the electronically locked door.

I wound my way through fifty or so fabric-covered grey-blue cubicles. My desk is located all the way at the back, where there is no natural light. It is, however, just four steps to the bathroom, and that's a big plus after having given birth to three children.

"Good morning!" My coworker Marley greeted me as I plopped down at my cubicle. She swiveled in her chair and looked at me. "Terrific coffee stain on your shirt." She turned back to her computer.

I looked down and cringed. My chest was a Rorschach test gone bad. Blue and brown make…well, mud. Had I been drinking orange juice, at least the colors would have combined to make an electric green, which I would have been ok with. Chalk up another reason to cut down on caffeine.

I took a napkin from my desk drawer and started wiping at the stain while Marley eyeballed my efforts.

As I worked my left breast, Rob Miller came up behind me. "Ha! Did you think if you watered them they'd grow?" I was blinded by the flash as he graced me with his perfect smile. He walked around me and sat at his desk.

Death Is A Relative Thing

This is why I come to work. It certainly isn't for the pay, which is substandard, and it isn't for the glory because being a support engineer is second only to being a dentist in terms of the number of happy customers you work with daily. It's for the people. My coworkers are also my friends, and as sad as this may be, it's the closest I come to having a social life.

Marley's a bit younger than I am and more manly than most women. She has long dark hair, short bangs and an 80s over-the-top manicure. She passes the time by tweezing chin hairs throughout the day while talking to customers. She does this without looking, which easily trumps my makeup application feats. Her clothing style leans toward loud flowing shirts, chandelier earrings and black elastic-waist pants. She's never been married and lives with a big multicolored parrot named Rodney that she believes suffers from teenage angst.

Rob is married with a young daughter. The family picture on his desk glows with three sets of perfect teeth surrounded by flawless complexions. I am convinced they're all holograms. Rob walks silently. I can never tell when he's heading around a corner or coming up behind me. He's tall and good looking in a clean-cut "boy next door" kind of way, and is one of the few men in town who is not afraid that being in my presence will be deadly. Rob and Marley do what I do, and we make a good team.

I logged onto my computer. There were 53 new emails, most of them too technical to read before noon and a third coffee. The first one I opened looked as though it had erroneously squeezed through the spam filter. After duly noting how much larger my penis could be in just five days, I went on to the next one.

"Hey, Marley. Take a look at this."

She joined me in my cube, squeezing in behind my chair so she could see over my shoulder to read the screen.

After a few moments she straightened up. "Are you going to go?"

"Don't know...you think I should go?"

"Rob, come here...check this out, April has a date!"

Rob ambled over and positioned himself between my desk and Marley. Cozy can be overrated and the oxygen exchange rate in my cube was rapidly decreasing.

"Ok, guys. I can't breathe!"

Marley moved partially out of the cube. "You're just nervous because you have a date tomorrow!"

"It is not a date! It's a meeting with a client."

"Yeah, but it is a male client from out of town. He wouldn't know about...well, you know." Rob's voice trailed off.

With a sigh, I swung my chair around to face him, aiming for his knee as I turned. "About what? That I killed a man by having sex with him? He was my husband for goodness sake! I could have bored him to death! Did anyone ever think of that? Truthfully, instead of running the other way, men should be lining up at my bedroom door to survive the experience as a show of virility! Heck, I should be making a fortune selling T-shirts that say 'I Climbed Mount April and Lived!' Maybe even hats and buttons..." I gave another deep, exaggerated sigh. "I don't even know what this guy looks like. He could be a toad."

The phone rang and I officially began my day. While listening on autopilot to a customer tell me how our software somehow chased his dog away and wiped out his bank account, I accepted the emailer's invitation to lunch via return reply. Jack Semenz, a customer I had worked with regularly but had never met, was an IT Systems Administrator. Divorced, with a daughter, he lived in Connecticut. His voice was warm and comfortable. That in itself was disconcerting, as I've found that people never look like their voices sound. He probably was a toad.

At five, I packed up to head home.

"Hey, lady, what gives!" said Marley. "Working half a day?"

"No, my mom and I are going out."

"That's nice. Girl's night out. Where are you going?"

I cringed, knowing I was about to be teased unmercifully. "A seminar. With a psychic."

Marley's tweezers dropped mid-pluck.

"Who are you going to see?" she asked.

"Steve Parker"

"Oh, my God!" Marley shrieked. "How did you get tickets to see him? I've been trying for months! You know, I went to a psychic once, and she told me that Rodney, before being reincarnated as a bird, was my brother in a previous life, which is why I feel so protective toward him."

She was breathing fast and little beads of sweat were launching a parade on her upper lip.

Oh, boy. "Look guys, I don't believe in any of this stuff. I'm just going because my father was smart enough to listen when my mother was talking, and that's not something I seem to have mastered. I kinda signed up for this without meaning to. Anyway, I have to leave. There'll be hell to pay if I'm late."

I picked up my travel mug, slung my laptop over my shoulder, and grabbed my purse. As I started down the narrow aisle between cubicles, Rob yelled out, "Say hi to Sal for me!"

Is it any wonder that I love these guys?

Death Is A Relative Thing

Chapter 3

"I always wanted to be somebody, but now I realize I should have been more specific."

— Lily Tomlin

My mother was at my door precisely at 7:00 p.m., her small body leaned in the doorframe, arms crossed, foot tapping. I prayed she wouldn't come all the way into the house. Every time she does, she gets some weird eye twitch, a dust rag mysteriously appears in her hand, and she threatens to throw out all my belongings. I left her there hoping for the best.

From the bottom of the stairs I called out, "Boys! Come here for a sec, please." I continued when they assembled. "Listen guys, I'm going out with grandma for a few hours. That means no girlfriends, parties, booze, drugs, joyriding, setting the house on fire, or otherwise having fun while I am gone. Got it?"

Scott looked at me. "What are we supposed to do then?"

"Try cleaning the front porch."

"Get the chocolate," said Brian.

I turned tail and headed to my car with my mother in tow. She stopped short of it and shook her head.

"No way!"

"What, Ma...?"

"No way am I getting into that thing!"

"Mom, it's not a thing, it is a car. C'mon, let's just go."

She folded her arms across her chest and I knew I was going down in flames. "That vehicle does not qualify as a car. It is an 'ar'...only part of a car." She settled into the Stallone battle stance, knees slightly bent, jaw jutting. The red highlights in her hair glinted in the moonlight. "There is no reason to take...that...when I have a perfectly safe all-American SUV we can drive."

I looked at the grey and black 1989 Suburban that she refuses to trade in. Considering its age, it's well preserved and real tough. A lot like my mother.

"But, Maaaaaaa." It never ceases to amaze me how the adolescent whine can creep right back into my vocabulary in a flash after 30 years of being mostly dormant. Worse than that, though, I realized I had made a mistake the moment it escaped my lips. With the whine, came a perfect opportunity for my mother to unleash the 'weapon.' The dreaded Sicilian Guilt Trip.

The Sicilian Guilt Trip is a time-honored tactic used by many Italian families, but my lineage has the most well defined version of it ever recorded. My grandparents, King Guiseppe and Queen Aida, honed the skill to perfection and used it with laser-like accuracy. My mother also has a very well developed version. I, unfortunately, seem to be missing the guilt gene entirely. Every time I try to evoke the power of "The Trip," my kids pat me on the head and smile as if I were a small child. My mother, however, was about to unleash it.

"So tell me, missy. Just what you would say at my funeral? Can you imagine all of the aunts and uncles huddled around talking about how you killed your poor ageing mother in that little mousetrap? They'll want to know why you insisted on taking your...uh...vehicle when we could have driven a nice safe two-ton SUV. How could you ever look your father in the eye again... and your brothers? And who, might I add, would do Christmas Eve dinner if I were dead?"

Ah, there it was... I could almost be ok with killing her, but Christmas Eve dinner was actually the clincher. Tradition and all that.

I walked to her SUV and climbed inside. It was huge and stopped just short of being a bus. She could, with one wrong move, take out a city block and not put a dent on the massive bumper.

The theater was only about 20 minutes from the house, but getting there did involve driving on the Long Island Expressway. From 5 a.m. until 7 p.m. on weekdays, that road resembles a large used car lot. After that though, the route opens up. I was glad of that, because my mother was going to need all the room she could get.

There was an uncomfortable quiet in the car for some time. I thought maybe I should talk about something that would put me back into her good graces.

"So mom, I have a lunch date tomorrow," I said.

The truck swerved wildly to the left and veered into the next lane as my mother turned her attention to me.

"Ma! C'mon, look at the road!"

With two fists and white knuckles she righted the bus again. "A date! Oh, April! That's great, honey….. Um, I guess he's from out of town?"

"He's a customer of mine who I've worked with off and on. He's from Connecticut and is going to be here for the day."

"Well, just make sure you take him somewhere that no one knows you, ok?"

I didn't have time for a snappy comeback because suddenly a car appeared in front of us and the truck stopped two inches short of it. Ahead of us, cars were lined up as far as I could see. No one was moving. "Mom, is all this traffic for Steve Parker? I mean it can't be, can it?"

"I told you April, he is very well known and very good. People come from all over to see him."

I watched the clock; 23 minutes later we had finished the final quarter-mile trek to the theater. I decided that discretion was the better part of valor, and did not mention that my Mini would have fit nicely in the breakdown lane and that we could have made it there 21 minutes sooner.

The theater was large, modern, and angular. Corrugated metal sheets, vividly painted with Steve Parker's logo, hung from the walls. Bright, multicolored spotlights traveled back and forth across the circular stage, met in the middle for a few moments and then began moving again.

Around the dais, thousands of seats graduated heavenward like bleachers in a stadium. I was glad we were seated on the ground floor. At least we didn't need a rappel line to go to the bathroom. We were only four rows from the stage and the man sitting in front of me, thankfully, was a sloucher. I looked around and there wasn't one empty spot to be found.

"What happens now?"

"Well, Steve will come out and do readings for some of the audience."

"Readings? Like what? Does he read palms? Minds? Tarot cards?"

"No, he talks to dead people who come through to him and relays their messages to their families. He's called a medium."

"And people believe this stuff?"

"Of course they do! You saw the crowds getting here! If they didn't believe it, why would they come here?"

Because they didn't listen while on the phone with their mothers?

I wasn't sure what to expect, but I had time to create a visual image of Steve Parker. I imagined him with a chiseled face framed by long black hair, a sexy pointed beard and a silver hoop earring just grazing the peasant shirt that was open to his waist, accenting a well defined abdomen. Billowing white sleeves and strong hands would be holding—nay, caressing a glowing crystal ball. His pants would be tight through the…

"Good evening, ladies and gentleman!" The emcee's voice boomed into the mike. "I would like to introduce to you the extraordinary and extremely talented, Steve Parker!"

Steve Parker bounded onstage. He was in his late fifties and, if round counts, had a very well defined abdomen. Contrary to my fantasy, Johnny Depp he was not. Humpty Dumpty may have been a blood relative.

His opening spiel was engaging and entertaining. He was quick to laugh and make the audience feel comfortable and I enjoyed his comments as he explained that he used his psychic ability to help others connect with deceased loved ones. When he was done, he looked around the theater, his gaze sweeping around the full 360-degree view from the dais as he took in the entire crowd. As he turned slowly, the audience grew quieter, almost still. The main event was about to begin.

On his second pass around the theater, he stopped directly in front of our section. I could swear his gaze fixed right on me. Indicating an area over by us with his hand, but staring at me, Parker said, "Over in this section, I am feeling something. The number four…maybe the fourth day, or the fourth month, or an age…. Does that mean anything to anyone here?"

A lady behind me raised her hand and announced that she had been four years old once. To the medium's credit, he didn't bite.

"No, no, that's not it. It's the number four, or the fourth month… I sense a man coming through… to talk to his wife… she is the four… Is this making sense to anyone yet?" He looked expectantly, almost beseechingly, out to the audience, and again, fixed his gaze on me. I looked away.

"The number four, the fourth month, the fourth day—hold on a second." He cocked his head to one side, apparently listening to some unseen entity.

Rolling my eyes, I leaned over to my mother and said under my breath. "You have got to be kidding me." I sucked wind as my mother elbowed me to keep quiet.

"The number four. He is also showing me an umbrella." Once again, he focused his attention on me. I could feel myself flushing under the gaze, and I didn't know why.

Without any warning, my mother stood up and started waving her arms like she was directing jumbo jets around the tarmac.

"Over here! Here!" She pointed at me, then grabbed my arm and tried to pull me to my feet. I stared in disbelief and horror. This could not be my mother.

With her hand still attached to me, I sank down as low as possible in my seat.

"Umbrella! April showers! My daughter's name is April and that is the fourth month! This is for her right? April! April….it has to be Sal! Stand up!"

"April, can you stand up please?" called Parker from the stage.

I slowly stood and hoped the roof would cave in on me or something equally convenient.

"Your name is April?"

"Yes."

"The fourth month and the umbrella…do you understand that?"

"Well, my mother does, so umbilically, I guess I do too."

The medium again looked as though he were listening to something that no one else could hear. "Your husband, he is dead, right?"

"If he isn't, he'd better have a damned good excuse for not renovating the kitchen."

"Hmmmmmm....he says he died having sex."

"He did."

"With you?"

"Yes."

Steve Parker took a few involuntary steps backwards, and every man within six rows of my seat started to sweat and hyperventilate. One skinny little guy two rows behind me went so far as to climb over his seat, falling into the lap of an elderly woman behind him. She let out a bloodcurdling war whoop and punched him square in the back of the head. I did a double take; sure enough, it was Mrs. Krupshaw! She gave me the finger.

Parker half yelled, "You're *that* April?"

Sigh.

Without moving toward me even an inch, and managing to compose himself, Parker continued. "He wants you to know that the leak under the sink in the kitchen needs to get fixed. It's causing a small flood in the basement."

"I don't have a leak."

"Yes, you do."

"No, honestly, I don't."

Steve shook his head as if I were a disobedient child. "Check it tonight when you get home. He's adamant about it." Parker "listened" some more. "He also says that you've been doing a great job with the kids and he's proud of you. He also wants to make you aware that your son is *not* in love with the girl who wears the thongs."

Huh? How did *he* know about the thong?

Steve looked deep in thought again.

"He also said to tell you '17317071.' Does that mean anything to you?"

Oh, yes. Yes, it did.

I startled myself by crying.

Death Is A Relative Thing

Chapter 4

"I don't believe in an afterlife, although I'm bringing a change of underwear."

— Woody Allen

It was late when my mother and I got to my house, which was quiet and didn't smell like beer or pot. So far, so good. My mother came in behind me.

"Mom, just sit. Don't clean anything, got it? I'll be down in a minute." I motioned to the couch in the living room.

I climbed the stairs to check the boys. Chris has his own room decorated in "post nuclear holocaust" style. He was asleep, so I turned off the TV and looked around, making a mental note to have his room sandblasted. Across the hall in the bedroom they shared, Scott and Brian were also asleep. To confirm I had to search for Brian under a mound of what I hoped were clean clothes. Scott was sleeping in something of a sitting position with his hands molded to the video game controller. I pried it from his hands and prodded him into a prone position, covered him with his blanket, and turned off the game.

I went downstairs. My mother was still right where I left her. No dust cloth, no mop! Unbelievable!

I had given her enough time to at least get the living room dusted, and had been kind of hoping she would squeeze in the kitchen floor too, but she was just sitting where I left her with a glazed look in her eyes. She followed me into the kitchen. I started two cups of tea.

"April, will you please look under the sink?"

"Mom, there's no reason to look under there."

"Just do it already." She looked at me. "You're afraid there might be a leak, aren't you?"

Maybe.

"Ma, if you're so interested in what's under the sink, you check it out."

"Hmph. Ok." She pushed herself up out of her chair and strode across the room. Leaning down she opened the cabinet and peered inside.

"Oh, for goodness sake, April! How do you find anything in here?" She got on her knees and started shoving dishwasher detergent, cleansers, paintbrushes, sprays of all kinds, and probably a dead cat out of the way. "Give me the garbage can… It is time to get rid of this stuff. Look at this, will you?"

"Ma! Leave it alone and come back here! I don't need the critique."

"No, I managed to get this far. Besides, someone has to look."
She was on her knees with half of her body in the cabinet, her butt
sticking out, reminding me that my mother has an exceptionally
well defined bottom. I craned my neck and angled my head over
my shoulder in an attempt to view my own, but was unsuccessful.
It hardly mattered. I knew somehow mine would be substandard
even without the visual. It was very sobering to know a woman
pushing 70 had a better ass than I did.

"Aha!" she yelled in triumph. "There it is! April, there is a
huge leak under your sink." She came back to the table and sat
solidly in her chair. "See, I told you the psychic was for real!" She
took her teabag out of her cup, smashed it smugly against a spoon
and deposited it on the napkin beside her.

"C'mon, ma. You can't actually believe in this stuff, can
you?"

She put her hand over mine on the table and momentarily
patted it in a motherly gesture that caught me off guard. "April,
honey, I don't know what is real any more than you do. But I
do feel that there is more to us than we understand. There was a
time that people didn't believe in germs because they couldn't see
them. Illnesses were considered a form of punishment for sins, and
society had to reorganize its view of the world to accept unseen
organisms as the source of their pain. This is the same thing, April.
Maybe we just don't understand how to see Sal yet."

"But mom, Sal, is not a germ." Well, occasionally he was, but
most often not.

"April, go look in the basement."

"No, ma."

"Why not?"

"Because I know all about the leak. I went down there two days ago and there was enough water in the basement to float a barge. I haven't gotten around to fixing the pipe yet, but I have duct tape."

"Ah, good, duct tape." She sighed with something akin to reverence.

I knew I had scored a few parental brownie points. Duct tape comes under the same exalted category as religion and clean underwear in Marie and Samuel Stallone's world. My father uses it for repairing reading glasses, lawnmower handles, and rips in the car upholstery. Once he even created a duct tape wallet that he used for two years before he disassembled it to fix a vacuum cleaner hose. Me? I only keep a roll in the house to make sure the kids stay in one spot.

While I finished my tea, my mother got up and rinsed her cup at the sink. I watched as she took the washcloth and cleaned the counters, swept the kitchen, threw out everything under the sink, and washed the kitchen floor.

Clearly, my mother was rebounding from the experience.

It had been a long day, and it was close to one in the morning when I finally headed upstairs, threw on an oversized T-shirt and got into bed. I lay there for a few minutes just looking around, waiting—for what, I wasn't sure. This was the one room that was completely different from how it was when Sal and I were married. I couldn't settle down in "our" room after his death; I needed to make it mine or I wouldn't ever sleep. It was now a deep gold, far from the sea foam green it had been in earlier days. I'd tossed the modern furniture and replaced it with deep cherry French provincial, and the colors were all rich and warm, with cranberry and dusky blue accents on the bedding, and the hardwood floor stained mahogany. I loved coming home to this cozy space. Being in there felt like being wrapped in a quilt, lounging in front of a winter fire. For a second I found myself worrying that Sal might not like the changes I had made, then realized I was concerning myself with whether a dead man approved of my color choices.

I spent a while tossing and turning with my mind in overdrive before I gave up and switched on the small glass bedside lamp. I walked over to the dresser to my jewelry box, opened it, and took out a small blue velvet bag. Back on the bed, I sat in the middle, opened the bag, and dropped the ring into my palm.

There were times, especially when Sal first died, that I would hold the ring all night in my fist and it would make me feel as if he were closer. It was a simple crosshatched white gold band that he never took off during the fifteen years we were married. I knew without looking what was inscribed on the inside.

17317071.

No one except Sal and I knew about the engraving.

Was Sal trying to communicate with me tonight? The engraving couldn't have been a good guess on Parkers part. I wasn't sure what to think of the whole experience. Like, how did he know about the thong? Heck, the only reason I knew was because I found it in the laundry. By process of elimination I concluded that it belonged to Chris's girlfriend, as it certainly wasn't mine and I was pretty confident that none of the boys had been sporting one lately.

Feeling kind of foolish, I said quietly—lest I give the kids ample reason to have me taken to a padded hospital room—"Sal? Sal, you out there?"

Nothing. "Sal? Maybe I should ask for a sign. Can you part the bathtub water or a burn a bush or something?" I gave it a second and thought it through. "You know, come to think of it, a burning bush would be a lousy idea. A little old-fashioned table rap or two would do the trick." I sat for a minute, waiting for a response, for any indication at all that Sal was in the room.

"Sal." I'm nothing if not persistent, "Are you out there?"

Silence.

I put the ring back in the pouch, closed it in my hand, and turned off the light.

It did make me feel as if he were closer. As I drifted off, Sal appeared in my dream. He straddled his jet black Fatboy, blue and white flames on the gas tank, revving the engine and gestured for me to climb aboard behind him. He looked like he did when we first met and I realized that this was a replay of our first date. He was a short stocky man with a rugged face even at 27. A five o'clock shadow by 3 p.m. always gave him a tough-guy look, but he was a teddy bear, super soft and squishy. We were on our way to see Dylan in concert on Jones beach.

I went to climb on the bike behind him, and fell off the bed. The scene vanished.

Chapter 5

"He was a great patriot, a humanitarian, a loyal friend; provided, of course, he really is dead.'

— Voltaire

Word gets around in an office as small as ours. The next morning I wound my way through the sea of cubicles to find my desk adorned with a large sign that read "Congratulations on your date! May he RIP." That was bad, but even worse was that with everything that had happened the previous night, I had forgotten all about the lunch meeting. I took a quick inventory of what I was wearing and realized that unless we were dining at St. Catherine's soup kitchen, I wasn't dressed too appropriately: jeans, a black cap-sleeve pullover shirt with two small bleach stains, and the infamous leather clogs. I sighed and pulled up my conference call calendar on the computer.

I had back-to-back appointments scheduled all morning. No chance of heading home and swapping out.

Marley, wearing black polyester bell bottoms and a button-down shirt that looked suspiciously like the fabric on my Aunt Linnie's living room wingchair, came back from the kitchen with two cups of black coffee. She deposited one on my desk. She slowly looked me up and down and her eyes rolled into the back of her head as she sighed.

"Did you work on dressing like you didn't want to impress?" she said. This coming from woman who owns twelve pairs of black polyester elastic-waist pants. "Good girl. Maybe he likes the seventy-fifth date look."

"Marley, I forgot all about it! I got distracted, I guess, by what happened last night."

"So, what happened?" Marley was working hard at looking like she didn't care, but she was dribbling a bit, so I know she was slightly more interested than she wanted to appear.

"Nothing much to tell you the truth," I said. "The medium was pretty good, and entertaining. He had a message for me, but he wasn't very specific."

Marley wiped the spittle from her chin with a napkin from my desk. "Well, how non-specific was he?"

"He said something about a leak under my kitchen cabinet, and knew about a thong that's been kicking around my house. He also threw out a few numbers I had engraved in Sal's wedding band. Like I said, not very specific. No big deal."

"What thong?" Rob asked over the cubicle walls. Of course I didn't hear him come around the corner. And of course "thong" was the only word he heard. I swear all men are hard-wired with selective hearing. Sex, beer, and buffalo chicken wings make the list. Virtually nothing else does.

"How can you say that's not specific?" asked Marley. "How can you get more specific than the numbers on your husband's wedding band?"

"Well, Marley, I'm kind of chalking that up to a good guess." Yeah, right. "Hey, come to the bathroom with me."

Rob peeked around and flashed his stellar smile. "Who, me?"

Gracing him with an eye roll, I turned back to Marley. "C'mon."

"Why?"

"Marley, C'mon. Please."

"April, what the hell do you need me to escort you to the bathroom for? You never go to the bathroom with the girls."

"Marley, please just come to the bathroom with me!"

Then the light dawned.

"Oh yeah, good idea," she said. We both grabbed our purses and headed to the ladies room.

The bathroom is long and narrow with seven stalls on one side and seven sinks on the other, with one long mirror running along the wall above. A hundred years ago the room was painted a lovely puke green, an intentional design concept dreamed up by management to ensure that no one would want to spend too much time in here.

Once inside, I bent over and checked under each of the doors. Perfect. No legs. We were alone.

"Marley, I don't know what to think." I began. I placed my purse in between sinks on the counter in front of the mirror and pulled out my makeup bag. "Steve Parker kept looking at me and talking to me, and he gave me those messages. He knew that I have a plumbing leak and that my son is not in love with thong-girl. The killer, though, is the numbers I had engraved into my husband's wedding band. I'm not sure how he could have guessed that. The whole thing has me freaked out. I even tried to talk to Sal last night! I feel like I am losing my grip on my sanity."

I was applying eyeliner and my hand was shaking so badly, I ended up looking like I had gone four rounds with Rocky Balboa.

Marley had been vigorously plucking all the while. It is impossible to believe that one woman could have so much facial hair. Sometimes I think she's part guinea pig. She didn't miss a beat tweezing while talking.

"What's with the numbers in his wedding band? Like, is it the date you got married?"

"17317071."

"What the heck is that?"

"Sal and I used to communicate a lot through pagers. We would send that message back and forth all the time. It says 'I love you' if you read the pager upside down."

Marley thought a moment and said, "I know that should be cute, but it makes me want to barf."

"It's the walls."

"Maybe, but probably not. April, how would Parker have known about that if Sal hadn't been talking to him?"

"I don't know…. It's weird. And then, it just seems so, well… *wrong* somehow. I mean, if Sal knows about the thong, does he know about other things? I mean, what if I actually have sex again someday? How can I possibly do it knowing that Sal is watching… or, worse yet, critiquing? Has Sal seen me in the bathroom? I may never be able to use the toilet again without some form of performance anxiety. I mean, we shared some bathroom things, but certainly not everything…. I'm just not sure I can handle the stress knowing he could be watching me 24 hours a day."

Marley handed me a wet towel. "Start over," she said. "You look like a mime."

I looked in the mirror, shrieked, and washed my face. I knew I should have put my makeup on in the car.

"Look April," Marley said. "I imagine that Sal has better things to do than watch you all day long, every day. My guess is that he is doing a bit of gambling, or chasing down a few halos and probably saying the occasional Hail Mary to atone. I am sure there are things he doesn't want to see, and wouldn't hang around for. As for sex…April, it's been six years, honey. If I were you, I wouldn't care if the whole damned town was watching!"

I laughed and gave Marley a quick hug. "Thanks. You're a good friend."

She smiled. "No problem. Anyway, I need to get back to my desk. I'm supposed to be on a conference call in about two minutes."

She took one last look into the mirror, yanked at a wayward chin hair that could only have grown in the last two minutes and led the way out of the bathroom.

The rest of the morning went very quickly. I talked to a few customers and conducted a number of useless conference calls that justified a few executive salaries. At noon exactly, Carl buzzed me at my desk.

"Heya, Sunshine, you have a visitor in the lobby."

"Ok, Carl, I'll be right there."

Marley and Rob stood to see me off. I took one last look in my compact mirror, fluffed my hair up a little, sucked my stomach in a lot, gave them both a high five, and headed down the aisle to the front of the building. As I passed by, another coworker yelled out "Good luck, April!" and seemed to be saying a novena for my date. I took a deep breath. I took the last few steps with my fingers crossed, pushed open the door to the lobby, and immediately laid my eyes on...a toad.

Not just any old toad, you understand, but a great big, incredibly warty toad. I could see right away that he was missing at least three teeth. He also looked like he was sporting the kind of aerosol hair that's advertised on late night TV. Worst of all, he looked at me like he wanted to snatch me out of the air with his tongue. I steeled myself, took a deep breath, and stuck out my hand.

"Jack, how...nice...to meet you." I added the best smile I could muster under the circumstances.

"Well, it is nice to meet you also," he said, sliming me with a handshake. "But I'm not Jack." He slowly looked me up and down while sticking his finger in his ear and quietly added, "Though I could be if you want me to be. In fact, I could be Little Bo Peep if necessary."

Carl gave a little throat noise and when I looked, he nodded to a chair closer to the front of the lobby. In it was Prince Charming. Whew! I wiped my hand on my butt in an attempt to dry off the toad jelly.

I was hoping the relief on my face was not too apparent as I walked over to Jack and stuck out my hand. He was good looking, hot even, with bronze skin and short light hair that held just a hint of grey and cut into a modified high-and-tight—very 'tough guy' but not too severe, a little longer on the top than would be regulation. His chin was strong, and his body belied his age. His nose was a little crooked but perfectly proportioned, and his eyes were incredible, a deep turquoise blue. Standing in front of me was an American icon, the modern-day version of Barbie's Ken.

"Hi, April. Nice to finally meet you." Ignoring my outstretched hand, with good reason I thought, he gave me a warm hug and a quick kiss on the cheek.

"Jack, you have no idea what a pleasure this is." I chanced a quick look over my shoulder and the toad was still there, eyeing up a wayward fly in the lobby. "I don't think I can possibly convey how much I mean it." It was then that I noticed how he was dressed: black Dockers, grey collared shirt, first button undone. Nice. And here I was looking like a bargain store end cap. I was tempted to explain why I looked so bad but I didn't want to scare him by confessing that I tried to converse with my dead husband most of the previous night. Occasionally I do concede defeat and bow to logic.

We walked through TCS's parking lot and when he saw my car he started gushing.

"A Mini Cooper! Red! Wow. I love these cars. I've always wanted to check one out. Look how much room there is inside! Is it a five speed? No! Six! Very nice. Do you like it? Is it fast?"

We had a pretty spirited conversation on the way to the restaurant centered on my car. I was happy about that because I love my car, and anyone else who loves my car is okay in my book. I was even happier, though, that we were not discussing anything personal. By the time we reached the Sea Basin restaurant in Old Port, I was feeling pretty comfortable with Jack and he was looking even more remarkably like Prince Charming.

I had decided against my mother's advice and took Jack to the Sea Basin because it's one of the few restaurants where I feel comfortable. Dressed as poorly as I was, taking him to an unknown restaurant could have been a complete disaster. The Sea Basin sits right on the harbor and has an old-time mariner feel to it, replete with ropes, anchors, and fake crabs hanging from the ceiling. From our table by the window we could watch the boats coming in off the bay. It was loud, comfortable, the food was great, and I could have worn a gunny sack and no one would have noticed. We ordered lunch and started munching on the breadsticks.

"So, Jack, what brings you down to Long Island?"

"Jeez, April! What is the matter with you?"

Huh? What kind of response was that?

"Well, I needed to go see one of my clients. He's in the next town over from here, so I went there first thing," Jack said. "I thought it would be fun to come see you. I can't tell you how helpful you are. You always fix my problems when I get you on the phone."

"Awwww...c'mon baby, look at this guy." Huh? *"He looks all apple pie and dumplings. Wouldn't you prefer hot, wet, and lathered?"*

God! That sounded just like Sal. I jumped and my chair skidded back a few feet, hitting the middle-aged woman seated behind me. She stared me down for a few seconds and I got the eerie feeling I'd seen her before. Then she gave me the finger. As soon as she did, I recognized her. Mrs. Krupshaw's daughter. Man, these people hold a grudge.

"Sorry," I murmured, then smacked myself in the head in an attempt to knock the voices out of it.

"I figured it would be a perfect opportunity to meet the angel behind the phone," Jack continued with a smile. He was doing a phenomenal job of pretending not to notice my behavior.

"Damn, what does he know about angels? Angels don't look like you, baby. Believe me, you are no angel."

Hey! What the heck was that supposed to mean?

I grabbed a breadstick, slathered it with butter, and started chewing loudly in an attempt to drown out the voice.

I smiled across the table at Jack. "That's nice. I always enjoy working with you too."

Our food came, which was a good thing because conversation is allowed to stop, or at least slow down, to allow for chewing. I mean, who wants to be seen talking with a wad of flounder in her mouth? It gave me a few minutes to think. What was happening here? Why did I think I was hearing Sal? Again, I am a little paranoid and a little more than neurotic, so I was beginning to worry that some of the more creative drugs I had taken in the

Seventies were doing some dance in my system and I was experiencing a flashback. I hoped this wasn't the case because the last time I did anything psychedelic I stripped naked and streaked the upstate campus of New Paltz College in broad daylight through two dorms, a jam-packed gymnasium, and the campus food court at high noon. A repeat of that deed with my current body would be a highly regrettable act.

"Hey, April, we need to talk."

"Huh?" I said to Jack.

"I didn't say anything." Ewwww, a food wad.

"April look, I need your help. Can you get rid of the yahoo over there so we can talk?"

I punched myself again. Jack was beginning to look a bit alarmed so I felt he was owed an explanation. In this case, I thought a fake one would be preferable to the truth, which was that I seemed to be holding a conversation with my dead husband.

"Look, Jack, I'm sorry. I fell head-first off a Ferris wheel as a kid and occasionally the wound gives me trouble. Today is just a bad day."

Jack smiled in the same way an adult indulges a small child or, more appropriately, an imbecile. "It's ok, April. I understand. We all have off days." He excused himself and got up to go to the men's room.

"Yo, baby! Hey, I need your help. You're lookin' good by the way. Except for the clogs."

"Sal?" I whispered. Nothing. Dead silence, so to speak. "Sal!" Still nothing. "Sal, I swear, if you're there you'd better start talking because I don't have much time."

"Nope, don't think you do, cause it won't take that guy much time to zip that teeny tiny thing up."

"Sal, this is crazy. Why do I think I'm talking to you? I'm beginning to be think I should be committed to a little rubber room and signed up for basket weaving classes two times a week. Where the hell are you?"

"Right here," said Jack, who had just come to the table. "Sorry, I didn't mean to take so long. The maitre d' stopped to talk. He asked if I knew how your husband had died. When I said no, he laughed and said I should ask you." He paused. "So, how *did* your husband die?"

I hate it when my mother's right.

"My husband died while having sex."

"With you?"

I nodded.

"You're *that* April?" Boy, it seems news travels.

I nodded slowly, expecting him to turn tail and run, but to my amazement Jack smiled, slowly leaned forward, and put his hand on mine. He said, "Well, killer, with a reputation like that, I hope I don't have to beat up all your of your admirers to get to your door."

I choked on my coffee, grabbed a napkin to clean up the portion that had come out of my nose and managed to mumble the words, "I think I could clear a path for you."

Death Is A Relative Thing

Chapter 6

"I do benefits for all religions. I'd hate to blow the hereafter on a technicality."

— Bob Hope

I dropped Jack off in TCS's parking lot and he kissed me on the cheek and promised to call. I had no intentions of going back to work. It was late—I had taken my allotted hour and then some—so I called my manager, Liza, and explained that I had food poisoning and I wouldn't be in for the rest of the day.

I drove back to the restaurant, parked facing the water, turned the engine off, and just sat. Sal and I had spent many hours at the harbor late at night. While we were dating we would pull up, turn off the old black Blazer, cuddle, talk, and occasionally give the back seat a workout. When the boys were small, on bad colic nights we would drive there and circle around until the kids fell asleep in the minivan, and Sal and I would cuddle in the front seat. Unfortunately our backseat days were over....the kids had taken over that real estate.

I was still confused about what had happened in the restaurant and was having a tough time breathing. I was beginning to think, or maybe hope, that I had imagined the whole thing. But in the safety of my car, I figured I could check it out and chance a conversation with no one.

"Sal," I said, feeling foolish. "Are you out there?"

"Yep, right here."

I turned my head to the sound and there he was. Sal was sitting in the passenger seat right next to me. Lord help me, he was still the most handsome man I knew, looking fine in his faded Levis, scuffed black leather riding boots, and Freedom Ride T-shirt. His receding hairline and his middle-age paunch had not deserted him in the hereafter and he sported the usual stubble. His eyes were greener than I remembered and I was mesmerized, just like the night we met.

I would have thought that if I ever encountered a ghost I would scream or run away, but this all seemed quite normal, which just reinforced the belief that I had crossed over into the land of straightjackets and rubber forks. But even that was ok, because I was just so damned glad to see him.

"Hey, Sal, you look good. A lot better than the last time I saw you."

He looked at me sideways. *"Very funny. You're looking good too. But Babe, the clogs have to go. What happened to the leather boots with the four-inch spike heels? Now those were sweet."*

"Hey, the clogs are comfortable. And the boots got thrown at the dog over in the McKinneys' yard. "

"That thing is still alive? Jeez, he has to be like 220 in dog years by now."

"Sal, what are you doing here? Can I touch you? Are you real?"

I reached out with my hand to feel his shirt, and in the place where my fingers seemed to touch him, his body faded away. I couldn't feel a thing. When I pulled my hand away, his clothing reappeared. I tried it a few more times before my brain accepted it as fact.

He looked at me and shook his head with a sad crooked smile. *"April, honey, you can't touch me. In reality, I'm not here. I'm just presenting myself like this so you don't have to talk to a disembodied voice. There isn't much to me these days—at least not in the way you're used to. I'm sorry. It's the best I can do, Babe."*

I felt tears start to well up behind my eyes. This was not fair! It was all so crazy.

Sal was right next to me and I couldn't smack him, get a hug, or feel his body against mine. Sigh.

"So, how come you didn't answer me last night when I was trying to contact you? I tried half the night. Instead you start talking to me while I'm out with a client?"

"A date."

"Client."

"Date."

"Client. But whatever, why not talk to me last night?"

"You know, April, if it was that easy to just bop from dimension to dimension, everyone would be doing it. There's a lot of planning and work that goes into a trip like this, not to mention the mounds of red tape. I couldn't talk to you last night because the approvals weren't completely in place yet. Believe me, the minute I could, I did. Of course, I was shocked at what I found. You eating lunch in our restaurant with a guy whose dick would fit in a thimble."

"Well hell, Sal, maybe I should have asked for measurements first! Hey! How do you know that anyway?"

"I hung out by the urinal."

Ack! "Do you do that often?"

"Not regularly. Listen, April, I need your help."

"What's the problem?"

"I got into a bit of a bind. I beat St. Peter at blackjack. He's usually a pretty cool guy, but somehow or another, and I certainly don't know how, I got caught using a marked deck of cards. Someone must have switched them out."

"You cheated St. Peter? Sal, what were you thinking?"

"I had no idea, April—I swear. The cards weren't mine!"

"Sal, you forget I was married to you. I've known you too long for you to get away with that line." I heard thunder in the distance and flattened myself against the car door.

"What are you doing?"

"If God decides to hit you with a lightning bolt, I don't want to be too close to the fallout."

"Look, Babe, this is the deal. I need to atone for this one. I need to do a few things here on earth, a couple of good deeds. Sort of like community service."

"What happens if you don't?"

"Oh, man...it's almost too horrible to say." My dead husband looked at me very seriously. *"I have to come back and remarry you."* He started laughing.

I leaned over to whack him in the head and my hand went through his skull and connected with the top of the seat, which was not very satisfying. "Well you are going to have to do better than that to get my help." I crossed my arms in front of my chest and pulled off a little toe tap on the floor of the car.

"Ok, April, this is the deal. I've had a restricted halo since I got to heaven. Most everyone gets off restriction within six months, when they figure out how it all works, but not me. I seem to be having a little trouble conforming."

"No, really? Go figure. So, Sal, just how am I supposed to help you?"

"In this dimension, I can't touch anything, and no one other than you can see me, so I need you to be the conduit I do my good work through."

"Sounds like I get to do all the work." I sighed. "So, do I score any brownie points for this? You know, with the big guy?"

"I can put in a good word for you."

"Great, a recommendation from a man who is failing Halos 101. I'll help you, Sal, but skip the letter to the boss."

"Babe, you're the best. I have to go now. I'll catch up with you later."

And just like that, he was gone.

I drove home slowly, wondering how crazy I was and whether a crazy person would know if she were crazy.

Death Is A Relative Thing

I wondered if my delusions would get worse. Would animals talk to me next? There's a lot of precedence for that sort of thing: Dr. Doolittle, Mr. Ed. Would I begin to exhibit alternate personalities? Become a kleptomaniac? I didn't know, but decided to stay away from visiting anyone for a while just in case their forks seemed more appealing than my own. I was calmer by the time I got home because I'd mostly convinced myself that seeing dead people wasn't at all like channeling or stealing, so if I was nuts, it was probably wasn't going to get worse…unless, of course, my great uncle Dennis decided to make an appearance. I didn't want to be the one that had to explain how his ashes got mixed with those of a female Jell-o wrestler. I walked into the foyer and was greeted by two inquisitive sons and a bouquet of flowers.

"So, Ma, who are they from?" asked Scott.

I picked off the card, noting it had obviously been handled and read prior to my arrival, but I refrained from accusing any of my offspring.

April. Thank you for a most interesting lunch. I would like to see you again. Maybe a little wine tasting this weekend? Call me. Jack.

I know I should have been thrilled at this prospect, but I was having a bit of a moral debate with myself. If I accepted the invitation with Jack, would I be cheating on Sal? I mean, dead is obviously open to interpretation. I stuck the card in my back pocket, thinking Sal would have a harder time reading it from that vantage point. And then I sat down just to make sure.

Chapter 7

"Life is better than death, I believe, if only because it is less boring, and because it has fresh peaches in it."

— Alice Walker

Saturday dawned bright and clear. I experienced no apparitions, out-of-body experiences, or visits from the dead for two days. I wasn't sure whether I should be relieved or angry. Deep down there was a little part of me that was irritated because my husband was ignoring me. Of course, most people are ignored by the deceased, and many of them by living spouses for that matter, but logic had never gotten in my way before.

Jack was coming from Connecticut via the Port Jefferson Ferry. I would pick him up there and we would head to the wineries on the east end of Long Island. I was wearing a pair of dress jeans, my tan cowboy boots, a cap-sleeved T-shirt and a tailored leather jacket. I skipped the belt, as I believe them to be servants of the devil. The boys were set for the day since had I left them a chore list; they would be so busy trying to figure out how to avoid the work they wouldn't be able to get into trouble.

The more time that passed without any sign of Sal, the more I believed I had dreamed the whole thing like a real-life Ebenezer Scrooge, and was beginning to think the experience had been caused by a substandard piece of shrimp. I was looking forward to the day with Jack. The trip to the east end of Long Island is a great ride, especially in the summer, with its expansive beaches and miles of farmland. Touring the local wineries is a favorite pastime of locals and visitors alike, but so far I had never done it. I was looking forward to the experience.

I leaned against the hood of my car and watched the ferry come in from the Sound into the bay. It was huge, one of the many that traveled between Connecticut and Long Island daily, each carrying up to 120 cars and three times that many passengers. It took some time before Jack descended. He saw the car, waved, and walked over. He looked good and I felt a funny little surge of activity in my lower belly. With a start, I realized that my hormones had just been dusted off and were kicking into gear. I just hoped that nothing was too rusty to work right.

There are a host of wineries on the east end, more specifically the north fork of the Island, so we pointed the Mini in that direction. Most of the little towns out that way have Indian names that are impossible to say or spell correctly like Nissequogue, Mattituck, and Aquebogue. They are replete with history, quaint Main Streets with unique little shops and friendly people. The road became more rural the farther we traveled into wine country. Long Island rivals some of the most distinguished wine producing regions in France as its climate and proximity to the water are very similar.

We stopped at *Trefal Wineries*. As we walked through the lot, Jack lightly placed his hand on the small of my back and the warmth spread quickly south. Again, it took me a minute to figure out what the sensation was. I seemed to have gone from a state of perpetual suspended sexuality to adolescent hair-trigger excitement without warning.

A portly gentleman with a disturbing resemblance to Orson Welles ushered us into a large room that had an understated elegance. A semi-circular bar fashioned from dark-stained barn board dominated the space, lit by copper fixtures hung from the ceiling. Wine barrels converted into tables with copper accents gone to verdigris dotted the room. Grape vines were painted in trompe l'oeil on the walls.

Jack said, "I'll go get a few glasses." While he waited for the sommelier to pour us some wine I gawked at the people around the room, about 35 of them standing about in small groups talking quietly. Most of them seemed well off, had bodies that clearly frequented tanning salons and tennis courts, and they tossed their heads often while talking. Jack came winding through the crowd with a great grin on his face. He looked perfect, comfortable with his surroundings, and I was glad to be with him.

"For you, Madam," said Jack, and with an exaggerated bow he handed me a glass.

I looked at the drink. "Is this it? This glass isn't even half full!"

He laughed. Raising his glass, he swirled the contents, then held the glass up to the light, then against the white napkin he held. I watched with interest. I hadn't told Jack that I had never been to a winery. Actually, I don't even drink wine much, as my tastes run more toward the inexpensive beer that is only sold warm in supermarkets. I was trying very hard, however, to seem at ease and, well, normal. After our rather odd first date I was looking to make amends. The others around us were swishing their glasses, too, looking at the liquid and laughing quietly amongst themselves. The atmosphere was low key, a little quiet, almost reverent, and I started settling a bit.

Jack was looking over a printed list of the wines available for tasting and made a little grimace. "It's a vertical tasting. Hmmmm, I much prefer horizontal."

I piped right in. "I know what you mean. I prefer horizontal also. I had to give up vertical about 20 years ago when I threw my back out so badly I was in traction for three weeks."

"April." Jack said gently, a smile playing on his face, "A vertical tasting is where all of the wines are the same type, but of different vintages. Finding the variances and nuances of each vintage is the challenge."

Just thinking about all this horizontal stuff was getting me warmed up a bit. I drank my glass of wine in one mouthful. Jack looked at me, smiled and touched his glass to his lips. Taking some of it into his mouth, he swished it around and then spit into one of the silver buckets on the bar. Momentarily horrified, I then noticed that others were doing the same thing. Sip, swish, spit.

"Oh, shit! I know what that is," I said.

"What was that April?" asked Jack.

"Jack, I just figured out what that thing is! It's a spittoon. I stuck a dollar in it before to tip the bartender. Guess no one is going to want it now!"

Jack put his hands on my shoulders, leaned down and gave me a quick kiss on the cheek. "I'm going to give Gillian a quick call, ok?" I watched as he walked away to call his daughter, shaking his head and laughing as he pulled out his cell phone.

Damn good thing I hadn't fished around in the bucket to get change. I walked away from the bar. There was just a lot of swishing and spitting so I moved out of the line of fire. I backed up a bit and ran right into Sal. Or through him, more accurately.

Blue polo shirt, tan Dockers, clean shaven. I almost didn't recognize him.

"Sal, what are you doing here?"

"April, your work-related meetings with under-endowed yahoos extends to weekends now? I sure hope they gave you a raise! Or hey, are you on a date this time?"

"Ok, Sal, you win, it's a date. You're dead, remember? It's good for me to get out once every six years or so. What's up?"

"See the guy in the corner? Grey button-down shirt, pasty faced and super-sized?"

I looked at the corner table Sal indicated and saw a disheveled man in his late thirties with a greasy black comb-over. Sweat beaded on his puffy face as he tracked the path of a well-endowed female guest, his eyes narrowing as they moved up and down her body. I felt a pang of disgust. He looked like a troll, like something that would sit under a bridge or peep through windows.

Death Is A Relative Thing

"His name's Earl. April, you need to get that guy to move out of the seat he's in."

"Huh?"

"He needs to move. You need to get him to do that—quickly."

"Why?"

"April, look, I have some good intelligence that if Earl doesn't move, he is going to get himself hurt or even dead, and the odds are seven to one against me that I can't get you to move him."

"Sal, are you telling me they have bookies in Heaven?"

"Ah, there you are," said Jack, handing me another glass of wine. He sidled up next to me and put his arm around my waist. "Gillian is doing fine. I'm a little overprotective sometimes. I just wanted to check on her."

I heard Sal: *"April, now please."*

I looked at the man across the room, then at Jack, then to Sal. I couldn't believe I was just put on troll detail by my dead husband. I sighed and excused myself. "Jack, sorry but I need to do something. I think it may be important." I gently removed his hand. "Look, don't forget where you were…. I'll be right back."

As I walked toward Earl, I became aware of a stench. He had sweaty vomit smell to him and he looked like he had been propped in his seat for more than one round of tastings.

He never saw me coming.

I knuckle rapped the table when I reached it. "Hey listen, Earl, I need you to get up from the table please."

He turned to the sound of my voice and locked his eyes on my chest. "Huh?" he asked.

"What the hell is he looking at?"

Nice to know Sal was right there by my side looking out for my virtue.

"It's not like there's anything to see."

"Damn you, Sal!"

The troll stared at me suspiciously with slightly unfocused eyes. "What? And how do you know my name?"

"Listen, I need you to move away from this table. Please just come with me."

"You want me to come with you?" He smiled slowly, displaying a few crooked yellow teeth. He pressed his ample self against the back of his chair to push away from the table and started to stand, but his belt buckle caught on the table, lifting it. A dish slid off and fell to the floor, shattering. People stared.

Earl raised his hands and said in his booming troll voice, "Hey! Hey, lady, you really want me to come with you?"

"April, you need to get him to move now!"

I couldn't believe this. From the corner of my eye, I saw Jack headed my way. Sal was yelling at me and the troll wasn't budging. I turned back to Earl. "Please, just follow me, quickly. C'mon, move it!"

I grabbed his arm and pulled.

"Oooh, you want it bad, eh hot stuff?"

I hadn't been called "hot stuff" in about thirty years. From anyone else it would have been a flattering lie, but coming from this blob, I felt nauseated. I yanked at him with all my might. He lurched off balance and his body fell forward, knocking over the table—and me. He landed on top of me. I gasped for air, realizing in horror as I fought to catch my breath that his weight was solidly on me and he had his face jammed between my breasts. His arms and legs were flailing wildly as he tried to gain some traction and I struggled to catch my breath. My hair and shirt were dripping wet. Maybe it was wine. I twisted my head to the side and came face to face with the spittoon. Maybe not.

The ceiling fan that had up until that point been whirring above his head started making a *whir-clunk, whir-clunk* noise and swung wildly. Everyone's attention was now focused above the table. The fan started spinning out of control and came down with a huge CRASH, with part of the ceiling still attached, onto the chair Earl had occupied moments earlier. "Holy cow! April! Are you ok?" Jack was above me, his hands underneath my arms pulling me out from under the troll. "I've never seen anything like that! How did you know it was going to happen? What is this stuff all over your...oh, oh boy..."

Attendants started flitting about offering assistance. I was given an official Trefal Winery shirt and shown to the bathroom so I could change and clean up. I turned the sink water on and dunked my head under without even looking. Some things are just better left alone.

I drove Jack to the ferry. When I got out of the car to say goodbye, he faced me and leaned in for a kiss. As I geared up to kiss him back I heard a voice yell, *"Remember the thimble, dammit!"* Distracted, I turned my head and Jack missed the mark. His lips met with my nose. I wasn't about to let this go. I grabbed Jack, readjusted the angle and kissed him, hard, defiantly. After thirty seconds or so, Jack pulled away with a noise similar to extracting a fish from a vacuum cleaner hose.

"Sorry," I said. "It's been a while."

"April, it's ok." He laughed. "I just don't know what to expect when I'm with you. It's good though. Fun."

We had been given six complimentary bottles of wine from Trefal. Jack took two of them and a container of blueberries we had picked up from a local produce stand and started walking to the ferry.

"Hold onto the other bottles for the next time we see each other!" He waved, blew a kiss and was gone.

I sat on my car and watched him go. "Sal? Sal? C'mon, Sal, don't I even get thank you? A pat on the back?"

"No way am I patting that back! I know where it's been and what was on it." He was sitting next to me on the hood of my Mini, dressed this time in jeans, T-shirt, riding boots and leather vest.

"Sal, another outfit? Are you paying someone to do your laundry up there, because as I recall, you had no clue how to run a washer."

"That is one of the beautiful things about heaven! I throw laundry in the hamper and it magically winds up in my drawers, folded ready to wear again."

"Hmmm, so heaven is a lot like being married, right?"

He shot me a sideways glance, smiled, and faded away.

Death Is A Relative Thing

Chapter 8

"The thing always happens that you really believe in; and the belief in a thing makes it happen."

—Frank Lloyd Wright

Walking through the lobby on Monday, I told Carl I was late because of the time differential between where the aliens took me and New York. I'm not sure he bought it, but I remained optimistic as I made my way to my desk. Marley turned in her chair to face me.

"Nice picture," she said.

"Huh?"

"Nice shot of you in the paper." In response to my blank stare, she handed me a copy of the *The End*, a weekly paper that caters to the North Fork wine-going crowd as well as the infamous Hamptons, situated on the South Fork.

Death Is A Relative Thing

Everyone on the eastern third of Long Island received the *East End Review*, which came out every Monday.

I looked in horror at the front page. There was a photo of me with fat boy's face in my chest and an overturned spittoon beside us.

"Ack!"

"So this is what I see first thing this morning? April, I thought you had a date with Jack this weekend."

"I did. He was there."

"April honey, I know it's been awhile, but here's some advice. You let the wrong guy get on top of you."

"Marley, it wasn't like that. I had to get this guy to move out of his seat. He fell."

"Okay, I'll bite. Why did you need his seat? Were there were no others?"

I dropped my voice. "Sal asked me to move him."

She stared at me for a moment. Her tweezers stood at ready and her right hand shook slightly. I could see it was all she could do not to pluck.

"Sal asked you?"

"Yes."

"*Your* Sal?"

"Yes."

"April, if Sal did talk to you—and I'm not saying he didn't, but if he did—why would he want you to move a fat, ugly man out of his seat?"

"Because of the odds."

"I'm not getting it," said Marley.

"I don't get it all either, Marley, but Sal is back. Well, he's still dead of course, but he's asked me to help him do a few good things here on earth to help him atone for a little trouble he got into up there. That guy on top of me, well, he was a good deed."

Marley gave a little laugh. "More like a charity case I'd say. Well hell honey, that ought to make up for anything Sal ever did and anything you are ever gonna do."

"Marley, this is all too much for me. In a way it's comforting knowing that Sal has been looking out for us, but, it's not like he's here. We can't build memories or be a family. I can't tell the kids he's around. That would be devastating for them and what's worse, this whole situation makes me feel like I'm cheating on Sal when I'm with Jack. I don't know what to do anymore."

"Have sex, you'll feel better."

"Actually Marley, that's part of the problem. What if Sal's a voyeur?"

"I don't know, I remember Sal as a 'do it yourself' kind of guy. I can't think he'd be on the sidelines watching. I get it though— it's freaky."

"Just a little." My phone started ringing so I turned into my cubicle and answered it. The caller was convinced that our software had not only blown up his printer, but was the reason his dog was having puppies and the cause of a sinkhole in his front yard. It was going to be a long day.

After work, I was cleaning up the dinner dishes when the doorbell rang. Three pairs of legs thundered down the stairs and I knew from experience that the boys were pushing each other in the stairwell and jockeying for position.

There were no war whoops of joy however when the door was answered, just revered whispers of greeting from the kids. If I needed any more confirmation that the visitor was my mother, it came via the sound of her one-inch sensible heels clicking down the hallway to the kitchen.

"So," she said, pulling a chair out from the table. "I went to get my hair trimmed today." She sat down and crossed her arms in front of her chest.

I looked at her hair. It didn't look any different than any other day: short, red, angry.

"Un-huh."

"While I was there Lillian brought me something to read. I was trapped under the dryer, you see."

"Uh-huh." Uh-oh.

"Do you want to tell me who I saw on the front page of *The End*?" She held it up to me and I made an effort to squint at the picture.

"Well, Ma, if you can't tell from the picture who it is, then I'm sure no one else can." I smiled widely, hopeful.

"April! I don't believe you. Could you just imagine how embarrassing this is?"

The walls around us had started to resonate with the sound of her voice and I realized that a new and improved version of the Sicilian guilt trip was about to be unleashed. I had to make a move to intercept.

I dropped my voice and said "Ma, it was all Sal's fault."

"Sal? Sal as in your dead husband Sal? Oh, April, you need to grow up and take responsibility for your actions.

I mean, I realize that your opportunities have been, well, *limited*, but you need to be a lot more discreet, and from the look of the guy on the front page with you, a hell of a lot more choosy."

Oh boy. I looked around the doorway to the kitchen and didn't see the boys. I needed to buy time and keep the kids from overhearing me. Moving to the bottom of the stairs I yelled, "Hey guys, next time someone comes down, please grab the garbage and take it out to the curb, ok?" That move well assured me that no one would venture downstairs until the next major holiday, or at least the next served meal, so I turned back to my mother.

"Sal came back. I mean, he's still dead, but he's been talking to me."

"April. Do you feel all right? I mean, the man's been dead for six years. He can't be talking to you."

Huh? What was that? "After all of the things you said about Steve Parker, you're going to tell me you don't believe me?"

"April, please. Anything is possible I guess. Ok, so where is he now? I want to talk to him."

"Ma, I think there's a rule. No one can see or talk to him except me."

"Well, that's convenient."

"I see she's as pleasant as ever." Sal appeared in front of me wearing a green-and-orange plaid kilt and sporting a set of bagpipes. A matching Tam o'Shanter covered most of his baldness.

"What the hell are you wearing?"

"Huh?" My mother looked around.

"Well, dammit, April, today is Kilt Appreciation Day, and you caught me in the middle of celebrating my Scottish roots."

"Sal! You're not Scottish!"

"Yeah, ok, so I'm not. But let me tell you, I sure am appreciating this kilt! You know that age-old question about what guys wear under these things?"

My mother had a worried look on her face. "April, what is going on? Who are you talking to?"

"It's Sal."

"Wow, April, your mother hasn't aged a day. Holding steady at what, 95?"

"Give me a break, April, it's not Sal."

"Ma, it is. Sal can you talk to her?"

"Nope. I made sure it was in the fine print." He reached one hand back searching for the pocket of his pants and then laughed. *"Don't seem to have my pants or the contract on me. But believe me, I can't talk to your mother."*

"ARRRGH. Ok, how do I get her to believe you are here?"

My mother crossed her arms in front of her body. "What is this all about April?"

"Mom, he can hear you, but he can't talk to you."

Sal said, *"Ok, April. Tell your mother that's a fine way to treat me after I kept her secret for so many years."*

"Ma, Sal says that you're not being nice, considering he kept your secret for so many years."

"Oh please! I don't have secrets! What's he talking about?"

"Ask her whose 34th birthday she forgot."

"Mom, Sal says to ask you who's 34th birthday you forgot."

My mother blanched. She put her hands out in front of her blindly, searching. "Sal? Is it really you?"

"Ma, whose birthday did you forget?"

"April honey, don't worry about it."

"Maaaa! Did you forget my birthday?"

"Awww, April, it was just a busy day, you know? Anyway, Sal reminded me in time."

"I remember that one! That was the year you came over pretty close to midnight. You brought me a donut with a candle stuffed into it, a can of cashews, a crossword puzzle book, and a cup of coffee."

"The convenience store was the only place open after ten. April, I am so sorry. Sal called when he realized I'd overlooked it. I swore him to secrecy."

"I can't believe you guys have lied to me for fourteen years?"

Sal looked at me. *"Only your mom has lied to you that long, Babe. I'm dead, remember?"* He blew into his bagpipes, did a little finger wave and disappeared.

Death Is A Relative Thing

Chapter 9

"Hovering between wife and death."

— James Montgomery (on his deathbed, when asked how he was)

Jack and Gillian were on their way to my house.

I don't know what I had been thinking when I extended the invite. It was Saturday, the weather was perfect, and I was flipping out.

"Brian!" I yelled. "Grab the hose and wash the paintball stains off the porch!"

"PMS week already?"

"Just clean kiddo." See? I could talk in three-word sentences also.

Chris walked over to me holding a few dead plants and said, "Mom, I don't see why my girlfriend can't come too!"

"Look, Chris, we've been through this. I want Jack to meet the family. In all likelihood, we as a collective unit are probably enough to handle in one sitting." I took a dried-out brown plant off his hands and wondered if watering it at this late stage would help. I was nervous about meeting Gillian. I had somehow made the first cut with her father, but this interview was the tough one: the *kid*. And a girl no less. What the heck did I know about girls? I was sunk.

I heard Scott yell, "Maaaaa, Brian got me wet!" Sigh. I walked over and stepped hard on the hose, successfully stemming the flow and proving to them both I still had the power. "Guys. Go get dressed!"

Scott was being a smartass and had pushed the hose between his legs. I removed my foot from it and headed inside, listening to him scream and his brothers laugh.

Upstairs in the bedroom I was confronted with the sad reality that it *was* one of the three PMS weeks I have per month. I worked to stuff myself into a pair of jeans that were two sizes larger than I should be and one size smaller than I needed them to be. I sucked in my gut and worked the button back and forth.

"C'mon April, just buy a pair of jeans that fit. Give it a break."

"Sal!" I was startled and lost my buttoning momentum. "Now I have to start all over!" I sucked in again. "And these do fit."

"When?"

"An hour ago."

"Mmmmhmmmm. Just a thought: your lips are blue. You might want to breathe."

I lost my grip again and was back to square one. I lay down on the bed, sucked in my stomach and finally buttoned and zipped my pants. The next challenge, of course, was to figure out how to get up now that it was impossible to bend at the waist. I started swinging my arms side to side in an attempt to gain enough momentum to bounce myself off the bed.

"Listen, Sal, you think you can figure out a way to get me off this mattress?

"Maybe, Babe, just give me a minute. I need to stop laughing first."

"Smartass!"

"What do you expect? I watched you swallowing a dozen or so Mallomars the other night."

"Hey, Sal, you forget what PMS is like?"

"Oh, no m'am! That's something no smart man ever forgets. Remember? I had three pounds of dark chocolate held in reserve at all times as personal injury insurance."

I rolled onto my stomach and by swiveling my hips back and forth pushed myself off the bed far enough to touch my toes to the ground. Launching myself with my arms, I shoved off and stood up.

"Damn, April, you're walking like you have your mother's broomstick up your butt."

"Sal, are you here for a reason?"

"Yeah. April, a few years before I died I sold a Jaguar to an older lady. I don't know if you remember her..."

"The one who said the car was a lemon? The one who kept calling round the clock for two months then tried to sue you? The woman who maimed you with her purse when she saw you in the supermarket parking lot? I believe that would be Mrs. Mitzner."

"Uh, yeah, Babe, that would be her."

"You know, she came to your funeral. She was kind of pissed I killed you first, but said she totally understood."

"I know. Very nice. Listen, I have always wanted to make that right. I was thinking that you could help me."

"What do you have in mind Sal? She insists you killed her husband. I'm not sure I can fix that."

"Well, looking back I should have gone over the car better but I swear I never thought it was unsafe."

"Poor Mr. Mitzner, having to be pulled out of the sump like that."

"April, I play poker on Tuesday nights with Morty Mitzner."

"Hmmm. Just wondering, did he get his halo?"

Sal ignored that. *"April, look. He just wants to get a message to Sadie. It might help my cause with you know who."*

"Sal, let me see if I have this straight. You sold a bum car to a lady and her husband, apparently without any remorse. You went through great pains to make sure you didn't have to fix the problem and very likely contributed to the death of her husband. Now you want me to give her a message that Morty's not mad at you so she shouldn't be mad either? And she will believe this because I'm going to tell her that my dead husband plays poker with her dead husband." I tried to take a breath. "Have I got it right?"

"April! What are you thinking! You can't tell her we play poker! She'd be royally pissed if she knew he was doing that." He paused for a moment. *"Otherwise, yeah, Babe, you got it."*

"Oh sure, Sal. She's going to believe me."

"Also, he wants her to know that she needs to see a doctor quickly. He says there's something wrong with her heart."

"What if she doesn't buy it?"

"Mr. Mitzner says to remind her of the time they 'did it' on the roof. Over the garage. He says she will understand."

"Yuck! Even I understand that! Too much information, Sal." I punted that around in my head for a minute but it nauseated me. "Ok, Sal, I'll think about it. Right now though, I need to get ready."

"Oh yeah! I'm looking forward to this party."

"It's not that much of a party, just Jack and his daughter. You aren't planning on hanging around, Sal, are you? I wasn't counting on that you know. Although, I do wish you could be manning the grill like you used to. "

He puffed out his chest and did a little strut around the end of the bed. *"Remember my homemade lime marinade? Everyone loved it."* He paused for a moment. *"April, I just want to be with the boys. I've watched them for years seeing them grow up, but it's different actually being here. I am so far away and usually they're, well, on something like a TV screen in my head for lack of a better way to explain it. It's nice to be so close."*

"But Sal, it's not like you can interact with them. I wish it were different, but we both know that won't fly. It would mess them up. And it might be a bit uncomfortable to have you here with Jack and his daughter coming."

"April, c'mon. Uncomfortable for who? You? No one else will know I'm here. This is important to me. I promise not to say

anything I shouldn't about what's-his-name or his unfortunate congenital genital disorder."

I sighed and my eyebrows went skyward of their own volition.

When Jack arrived with Gillian he scored immediate brownie points with the boys as he swung a yellow Porsche Cayman S into the driveway.

My three sons moved their heads in choreographed perfection, panning the car from front to rear. Their mouths hung open and Brian had a bit of an eye twitch going. They stood that way, entranced with the car until the passenger side door opened. A female leg emerged—long, bare and tan. They collectively shifted their attention to Gillian and I heard Chris suck in hard.

"Oh. My. God." He watched, transfixed, as Gillian eased her eighteen year old body out of the car. She had long dark hair that fell almost to her waist. She wore a heather grey baby doll tee paired up with denim shorts. Her toenails shone a summery pink and she wore a turquoise toe thong on the right foot. She had huge green eyes and wore just a hint of makeup. She didn't need much. She was stunning.

"Oh my God," said Chris again, and this time I could have sworn he genuflected while he murmured a small thankful prayer. I was quite excited about his reaction. After 20 years, my son had finally found religion. My mother was going to be so happy.

Jack was walking around the car toward us, smiling, with one arm gesturing to me and the other around Gillian.

"You know what they say about guys who drive cars like that don't you? Penile extensions..."

I mentally head-slapped Sal, gave Jack a quick kiss on the cheek, and stuck my hand out to Gillian.

"Hi, Gillian. I've heard so much about you. I'm glad you were able to come."

She took my hand "Same here. My dad tells me you're a pretty funny lady."

Before I had time to process that, the boys came up from behind. Chris looked at me expectantly. I took the hint.

"Gillian, these are my sons Scott, Brian, and Chris."

Scott and Brian both shook her hand a little shyly. Chris, however, being about as much a ham as a person could be without actually being cured and smoked, didn't hesitate for a moment. Looking her straight in the eye, he reached out and shook her hand and, without letting it go, said, "Let me show you around." He steered her to the backyard.

"Smooth," said Jack, his eyes tracking his daughter.

"Just like his old man."

"So your husband was a bit of a charmer? Well, I can only hope he was also a gentleman."

Oh, boy. I blanched and mumbled, "Uh, yeah," and broke out into a trot to catch up to them. They went straight to the lawn swing and sat down together.

"Do you need me to do anything? I grill pretty well," said Jack. "I can pull together a mean lime marinade if you need."

I heard Sal choke, and snort out, *"Hmph!"*

"Maybe next time. The steaks have been marinating for a few hours already. Follow me. I have everything ready to go in the fridge." I walked up the back steps and through the door that led into the kitchen. As soon as we got inside, he put his hand on my hips and turned me around to face him.

"I've missed you," he said. He leaned in and kissed me full on the lips. He tasted great and I was in no hurry for it to end. My eyes closed and my mouth opened.

"Oh, god, how gross. April! C'mon already. This is my kitchen. What do you think you're doing? Besides, you are about to get a visitor. You want to get caught necking with microphallus here?"

I pulled away, scowling. "Someone's coming?"

Jack looked confused. "Are you expecting someone else?"

"No, but I have a feeling…"

The doorbell rang.

"Wow, April, that's a good trick, knowing *before* the bell rings."

"Jack, excuse me. I'll be right back."

I went to the front door and opened it. Standing on the front porch was my mother, looking a little like a bruise with her bright red hair and blue sundress.

She was holding a bakery box tied with red and white string. "Pineapple cheesecake," she said, craning her neck to look around me into the living room.

"What brings you here?"

"The party of course."

"Ma! It's not a party. Who told you about it, because I know I didn't?"

"Of course you didn't. I had to find out from the girl who does my nails."

"Huh? How did she know?"

She pushed the box into my stomach and I took the handoff, but not without anticipating a sidestep. Unfortunately, I expected she would scamper by to my right, but she dodged past me on the left in a surprise victory dash and made it into the living room.

"She knew because her sister works with Aunt Anna. You remember Aunt Anna right? The one who was arrested two Christmases ago for allegedly fondling an elf in Fellow's Department Store downtown? I still think the charges were bogus. I mean she couldn't have bent down like that, not with her arthritis being so bad. Anyway, she's the veterinary tech for the animal hospital that takes care of Marley's bird. I mean, really April. If it weren't for horrifying newspaper photos and mutual friends, I would never know what goes on in your life." She paused momentarily. "Where is he?"

"Who, me?"

"No, not you," I said.

"Not me what?" asked my mom, then the light dawned. "Ohhhhh, him. What does Sal think about your date?"

"He has no say in it." I sighed, knowing my mother wasn't about to leave. "C'mon mom, I'll introduce you to Jack."

In the kitchen, Jack had pulled the chicken and steaks from the refrigerator and was turning the meats in their respective marinades. He smiled at me and then looked at my mother.

"Jack, this is my mother, Marie Stallone. Mom, this is Jack."

"Oh, April, he is so much better looking than that guy who landed on top of you in the winery. Jack, did you see that picture in *The End?* Probably the least flattering photo I've ever seen of April."

She leaned over the table and took his hand in a choke hold.

"Well," Sal chimed in, *"there was that picture from Rob's wedding where you had tucked the back of your dress into your pantyhose. Remember? You were halfway through the Chicken Dance gyrating your ass all around before we were able to alert you! What a sight! The photographer made great use of that wide angle lens though...."* I groaned, making a mental note to address this with Sal later. My mother looked at me funny and then turned her attention back to Jack.

Jack laughed. "Yes, well, it turned out to be a fun and interesting day. We got some free wine and April got a T-shirt, so all in all, it went well." He gently extracted his hand from hers, adding, "Very nice to meet you."

Jack manned the grill perfectly. As usual, I had a lot more food than was necessary. It's an Italian thing. I'm genetically programmed with an overwhelming need to feed. In my family, how much food you place on the table is in direct proportion to how favorably you think of the guest. It's better to have a week's worth of leftovers than not enough food. In fact, I hyperventilate and have to breathe into a bag if I think I'll be so much as an olive short at dinner.

My mother and I were taking food from the refrigerator to bring outside.

I handed her the ketchup, mustard, relish, a few varieties of salad dressing and mayo before she started rummaging through my cabinets looking for something to put it all on.

"What does Sal think about you having Jack over to the house?" she asked pulling a round pizza pan from the cabinet.

"Ma, what can he say?" Well, actually he always had something to say, but I wasn't going there. "He's dead. No one can have a relationship with a dead man. Well, unless of course you count Aunt Lucy, but truth be told no one could blame her for not noticing for so long." As far as anyone knew, my Uncle Mike hadn't moved from the sofa for a solid three years before his death; it wasn't really her fault.

I helped her put the stuff on the makeshift tray and took the salad out of the fridge. We went through the back door and made our way to the tables on the patio.

"Well, I hope he remembers he's dead and you have to go on with your life," my mother said.

"You know, there was a time when I thought that I'd be rid of her if I was dead. I took some solace in believing it could be true. Now I realize it was only a cruel fabrication. It's almost as disappointing as the day I found out magazine centerfolds are airbrushed."

I looked to the voice and there was Sal, standing under the umbrella between Brian and Scott. He had on a blue Hawaiian shirt with a huge red hibiscus flower on the front paired with yellow Bermuda shorts that I knew from experience he had buttoned under his belly, and he was wearing a straw colored panama hat. The drink he was holding came with a little multicolored umbrella that he twirled between his fingers. I was startled though, by the huge pink flamingo he was leaning on. At first I thought it was plastic, until it craned its neck, looked at me and winked. I tripped, losing half the salad to the deck before I was able to compose myself.

Death Is A Relative Thing

There were a few tables with chairs set up on the patio. Chris and Gillian chose seats alone together at the small square table furthest away. The rest of us sat at the large table under the awning and started passing the food around.

"So, when does school end for you guys?" Jack asked Scott and Brian.

"What the kind of a stupid question is that? It's the last week of the school year. Those two haven't stepped foot in a classroom in three days."

"Huh? What the hell? Scott! Brian! Have you been skipping school?"

They quickly glanced at each other and Brian said, "No way, Ma!"

Jack said, "Wow, April, that was a leap of logic."

"Yesterday they were at Wet and Wild, the water park right over in Statsberg. Look at Scott's hand. The stamp wouldn't come off completely in the shower. Why do you think it's been in his pocket all day?"

I had noticed his hand was buried, but that's not unusual for any of the boys. They were always making sure the parts were all still there.

"Oh, I'm sure they wouldn't do that," said my mother.

"You're kidding, right mom? I wish you had been that understanding when I was a kid. Scott, let me see your hand."

He looked around the table and, seeing no one that would save him, he held his left hand out in front of him.

"No, Scott, the one that's been playing pocket pool all day." His hair, usually standing on edge in a spiky cut, started melting.

He shifted from side to side in his chair and then took his right hand out of his pants.

I grabbed it and pushed it to my face. One day I'll admit I need glasses. Sure enough, I could just make out the faded letters WAW. I stared Scott and Brian down. "You guys are unbelievable! Needless to say there's going to be a chore list associated with this."

The two of them exchanged glances, wondering how I could possibly have known. I think it's important to make them believe I have mad mommy skills, so I just smiled as a reminder that I will always know more than they think I do.

After dinner my mother helped clean up. She peeked out the kitchen window at Jack and then turned to me. "April, you need to hang onto this one. He's a keeper."

"Ma, Jack is a nice guy, but we still need to learn a lot about one another."

"Well, have sex. That will sort it all out. You learn everything you need to know in a short period of time."

Huh? "Mom, do you realize that not only did you stick up for the boys, but you've suggested I have sex? And both of these miracles occurred on the same night? Of course the sex thing is a little creepy coming from you but is there an epiphany or something going on here I should know about?"

"No, April, just making sure you don't let this one slip away."

"I'll do my best mom."

It was exactly 7:00 p.m. when my mother left; any earlier and she would have had to call me.

Scott and Brian excused themselves to go to the mall with some friends soon after that. Eventually Gillian and Chris made their way over to the table where Jack and I sat.

"Hey, Dad, is it ok if Chris and I take a walk?" Good move, always send the girl in to ask daddy.

"Where?"

Chris jumped in to help. "We have a great lake about a block from here. Sunset on the beach is beautiful. I think Gillian would like it."

I could tell Jack was struggling. He wanted to be alone with me, but he didn't want Chris to be alone with his daughter. Smart man. Then again, he looked over my way for help, so maybe not so smart.

"She'll be fine with Chris... uhhh, right Chris?" I stared him down.

"C'mon, Mom. Gimme a break."

Turning to Jack I said, "They'll be fine. It is beautiful down there—let them go. Maybe you and I should take a walk and join them in a bit. I think you'd like it, too." I figured that was enough of a monkey wrench to throw in the works. If they were looking over their shoulder for us every two minutes or so, they'd have to at least stay dressed. "That would be okay with you guys, right?"

"Uh, yeah, sure Ma."

"Be back in an hour," said Jack.

We watched as they left the backyard.

"Alone at last!" We said it in stereo and laughed.

Jack and I brought the last few items on the table into the kitchen.

I was covering the fruit salad with plastic wrap when I felt his arms circle around my waist. He leaned into me and nuzzled his lips against my neck. I was beginning to melt and it had nothing to do with the warm weather. I turned and faced him.

"You realize," he said, "that we have the house all to ourselves. Now, what trouble can we get into in, say, an hour or so?"

I was going to say "about the same amount of trouble our kids could get into," but I figured that would merely spoil the moment so I chose to say nothing.

I was backed against the sink. Jack's mouth was locked on mine and his hands began to wander around my waist, inching up under my shirt. One hand was on my back, the other exploring the front. He found my breasts and pushed me up against him harder. I sighed as his tongue ran down the length of my neck. I moved my hands up his chest, then slowly made my way down around the waist of his pants.

He felt good, great in fact. I hadn't been this close to a man, felt this sexy, or horny since...

"April, what is this fascination you have with the kitchen? My kitchen?"

I startled and the moment was broken. I willed Sal to go away, but he didn't budge. I slapped myself in the head trying to get him to leave.

"C'mon, you're gonna get all hot and heavy and then deal with the little penis thing? Are you ready for that kind of disappointment after all these years?"

"Stop that, dammit!" It took a second before I realized I said it out loud.

To his credit, Jack stopped. His hand stayed on my breast, but he pulled his mouth away from my neck.

"April, are you ready for this? If you're not…"

Damn you, Sal. "Oh yes, Jack, I am, truly I am."

"Mmmmmm, good." He leaned into me again. "From what I understand, you have a reputation of being killer good in bed." He smiled and then moved his tongue down farther, tasting me, moving his lips to the top of my shirt.

"April, c'mon. Killer good? It's not like you weren't decent in bed, but let's face it, we were married a long time. I'm pretty certain it was the Julia Roberts triplet fantasy that put me over the edge. Pretty Woman *times three would kill any man!"*

My passion had almost completely drained. How was I going to do this?

Sal was right here and he was my husband, albeit dead. I felt like I was like having group sex with none of the benefits.

"Jack, could you just wait here for one minute please?" I extricated myself from his arms and, ignoring the confused looks, walked out of the kitchen, through the living room, into the front hall. "Sal!" I whispered. "Sal!"

"Heya, Babe!" Sal appeared before me wearing his bowling shirt, the one he had bought when he was twenty-five pounds lighter—blue with a black stripe down the middle. He was juggling three bowling pins and was sporting a full head of hair combed into a circa-1950s rooster tail.

"You have to be kidding me. What did you have to do to fit into that? And who did you have to pay off for that wig you're wearing?"

"First off, it's my own hair." With one hand he grabbed a fistful and pulled, hard. It didn't budge but the cool thing was that he kept the three pins in the air with only one hand. *"I told you, I look like this because you can understand it, but hell I can look like Marilyn Monroe if I want to—although last time I did that, she got pissed because my legs looked better than hers. But that's not the point, I guess."*

"I remember when you dressed up like a Playboy bunny the Halloween I was pregnant with Scott. It's true. You've got great legs." I sat on the bottom step of the stairs and put my head in my hands. "Sal? What am I going to do? I like Jack a lot and I want to explore this relationship. If you hadn't shown up it would be hard enough because I always think about you. You've always been there, in the back of my head. But now, you're right in front of me. You've taken center stage. How am I supposed to do this?"

"Babe, this is hard for me too you know. You think it's easy for me to watch you fondling another man? I want to just deck him for, well, for kissing my girl. But I do understand how tough this situation is." He was quiet for a second. *"Listen, I'll go away if it's easier for you. I've gone this long on restriction."*

"Sal, you know I'll help you. I'd never leave you halo-less."

He smiled broadly. *"Babe, you're the best."*

"Yeah, well, in return, I could use some space if you don't mind. Can you please just leave now? For a little while?" As I said it, Jack turned the corner from the living room into the front hall.

"April. What's wrong?"

"Nothing Jack, nothing."

"Then why are you telling me to leave?"

"I wasn't talking to you!"

"Then who were you talking to?"

I stood there, looking like a deer caught in the head lights I'm sure. He sighed and sat on the bottom step.

"April, you need to trust me if we are ever going to build this relationship."

"Jack, believe me, you won't believe me."

"April, I can tell you're having a hard time and we need to talk about it."

I took a deep breath and jumped off the cliff. "I was talking to my husband." Jack got very quiet and I realized it was a long, lonely way down.

"The dead one?"

"Well, if it helps any, he's the only one."

"It doesn't, but stay on topic. Are you feeling guilty about having a relationship with me?"

"It's a little like that, yeah." I didn't know how much of this he could handle but I was about to find out. "Look, Jack, Sal talks to me and I'm finding that a little disconcerting when we're up close and personal and contemplating doing anything sexual. I mean, that's where we were headed, right? Unless I got my signals crossed it, I think there were only a few articles of clothing between us and the bedroom, or the couch or the kitchen table for that matter."

"Kitchen table?" Jack smiled. "Sorry, I got sidetracked for a second there. Look, even though he's been dead for six years, April, I'm sure you've anticipated being in this situation and thought that you may feel a bit, well, like you're not being loyal."

"Well truthfully, given my reputation with men, I haven't thought that much about it."

Jack smiled and said, "Yeah well, I don't think what you're feeling is unusual."

"Yeah, Jack, but it was easier before Sal popped back into my life. Now it's more difficult because when he talks, he's right inside my head. Not only that, but he's right next to me."

"So, you aren't just talking to him, you hear him talking back?"

"Well, yeah. It's complicated. See, he hasn't been able to earn his halo in all the time he's been in heaven and he screwed up big time with St. Peter. Look, it's a long story."

"Damn, April! You have to stop telling people. We've almost hit quota."

"There's a quota?"

"Yeah, five total for the visit and preferably less. So far your mom, Marley and now this guy knows. You can't even tell all the boys if you choose to…"

"C'mon Sal, you should have told me."

"April!" Damn. I'd forgotten Jack. He reached out and gently took my hand in his. "April, dead people can't talk to live ones. Do you know how crazy that sounds?"

"I know, it seemed that way to me, too, but it's true, Jack."

"Well, if it is, there's no way I can compete with a ghost."

We heard the kitchen door slam. "Ma! Where are you?"

It was Chris. "Front hall. Be right there."

Jack looked at me for a long minute and I could tell he was struggling, deciding what to do next. He shook his head, gave me a hug and gently kissed my cheek. "Listen April, I want to be with you. We have a lot in common and could be good together. But that won't ever be able to happen unless you leave your past behind you. You have my number. Call me if you think you can get to that point or if you think I can help you get there. But I'm not going to push you, April. This needs to be your choice."

I didn't know how to make it right, so I didn't try. I walked them to their car. Chris was holding Gillian's hand and out of the corner of my eye I caught them exchanging a quick kiss.

"April, I hope this isn't goodbye," Jack said. He hugged me and got into the car with Gillian. It certainly felt like the end as the pit of my stomach sat between my knees. I watched him pull out of the driveway and head down the road. Chris smiled and waved. I wished it were that easy for me.

Chapter 10

"**My only fear of death is reincarnation.**"

— **Tupak Shakur**

"April, I don't have much time, but I need to talk to you."

Ugh.

Looking around I said, "Sal, I thought you were going to give me some space."

"It's been two days. Besides, we need to talk."

"Where are you?"

"Not today ok? Can't we just talk?"

"Sal, please. I much prefer to see you."

I heard him sigh and then he appeared. His hair was long, spiked, and platinum blonde. He wore leopard-skin-print bell bottom jeans and a satin long-tailed tux jacket that did nothing to hide his midriff paunch. High-heeled black leather platform boots and a blue-edged Les Paul guitar that hung from his body by a fluorescent yellow strap completed the ensemble.

"Babe, before you say anything, this is solely for extra credit. The band entertains on the plaza once a week or so and I get a few community service points. This week it's heavy metal, next week it's swing. I never knew heaven was so into music. We need to make this fast because I'm on a super tight schedule."

"When the heck did you learn to play the guitar?"

"We don't play, it's all lip synching, but heck, we have fun."

"Amazing, you wouldn't have been caught dead in that outfit in real life."

He looked at me a little funny and continued. *"Look April, you have a problem. The guy you saved at the winery—well, he was slated to be with us by now. Well, probably not us, more like downstairs, but regardless, he isn't supposed to be walking around. He was a big cheese goon in the Fenders, which is a local gang. Rumor has it that he fell into a bottle and started making bad decisions. I didn't know, but his was a contract hit."*

"What does that have to do with me?"

"Well, the picture of you on the front page of The End got around to some bad people, specifically Joey the Cook. They're pissed you botched up their job. Word on the street is that they're gunning for you."

"Joey the Cook? What the heck kind of a name is that?"

"I don't know for sure, but rumor has it that he's pretty good with a knife and makes a killer zucchini bread. I don't think I want to find out if it's true. I hate zucchini."

"Ok, so, Sal, they're going after me? Because, might I remind you, you're the one who told me to save that guy."

"Yeah, well, bad intel I guess. Anyway, I'll keep an ear out here, but maybe you should stay inside and don't let anyone see you and get a mean ass dog or something. Oh, and lock the doors."

"I'll keep it in mind, Sal, but I'm not about to hide out. I mean if the original info is bad, this could also be wrong, right?"

"Babe, listen, I would never forgive myself if something happened to you. Please be careful."

Great. My life was now officially a soap opera. I promised Sal I'd watch my back.

The Saturday after the barbeque I was heading to Marley's apartment. I had asked her to go to Mrs. Mitzner's with me, because, well, the idea of talking to Mrs. Mitzner scared me. Marley lives in a small apartment complex one town over from mine.

I parked my Mini in front of her building, went inside and knocked on her door.

"Come in!"

I tried the door, but it was locked.

"Marley, it's locked!" After waiting for a minute I knocked again.

From inside I heard, "Come in!"

I yelled louder this time "Marley, I can't! It's locked." A door down the hallway opened a crack, and an ancient old man with rheumy eyeballs and a bulbous red nose peeked out, assessed me, then closed the door. Creepy.

Once more, I heard, "Come in!"

The door still wouldn't budge so I rang the doorbell. This time Marley opened it. Her long hair was pulled into a bun and she wore polyester bell-bottom jeans with a pair of 70s platform shoes. She had huge sterling silver hoops in her ears.

She stood there and stared at me for a moment before moving aside to let me in. Someone said, "Come in!"

"Hey! How did you say that without moving your mouth?"

She looked at me uncomprehending for a moment and then started laughing. "Rodney."

Mental head slap! I had forgotten about the bird-brother.

"He can talk like that? Amazing."

"Yep. He also says 'Hello' and 'Your ass is itchy.' I make him answer all the bill collector calls. Anyway, glad you asked me to come with you. I need to get out of the apartment. Rodney's been rather exasperating lately, sleeping until noon, tossing his food outside his cage, yelling for no reason. Boys will be boys and, well, I know how teenagers are but it's good for me to break away."

And I thought I was weird talking to a dead guy.

It was eleven in the morning and already 80 degrees. I was sweating before I even got near Mrs. Mitzner, making me pretty sure I was just going to become a puddle when I did get closer. I was convinced I wasn't going to be invited for tea in the garden, and I prepared myself for the worst. My nerves were raw. The long cobblestone driveway led up to a meticulously kept large green and gold colonial. Cherry trees dotted the front lawn and a white wrought iron fence defined the property line with understated elegance.

"Are you ready?" I asked.

"I think it's sweet," Marley said, "that Mr. Mitzner is worried about her, from the other side."

"Ya think? Marley, think this through. He's playing cards with Sal. My guess is that he doesn't want her dropping dead of a heart attack and prematurely busting up his game."

"Cynic."

I smiled and knocked on the door. There was a lot of rustling and bumping, footsteps in the hall, and then the door opened as far as the safety chain would allow. A brown eyeball stuffed under a wrinkly blue shadowed eyelid peered through the space.

"Mrs. Mitzner?"

"April Serao!" she hissed. "What are you doing here?"

The door slammed shut. I waited for a minute expecting it to reopen without the chain. When it didn't, I knocked again. "Mrs. Mitzner! I need to speak with you." There was more rustling from the inside and the window curtains were drawn closed.

"Mrs. Mitzner, Marley and I came to talk to you about your husband. Can you please give us a few minutes of your time."

The door opened again the width of the chain. She clenched her jaw and spoke through the space between her teeth. "Shush yourself! Now is not a good time. Just go away."

I love being shushed so much that accidentally I got exceedingly loud. "Mrs. Mitzner, we've got to talk to you. It's about Mr. Mitzner."

"SSSHHHH! SHHHHH! Hold on a minute!" The door slammed shut and I heard it unlatch. Mrs. Mitzner stepped onto the front porch.

"Keep your voices down." She looked over her shoulder and back to me again.

She was wearing a robe, black, short, and satin. There was no mistaking the thigh-high leather boots.

I sneezed. "Mrs. Mitzner, I'm not sure how to tell you this, but I received a message from your husband." I sneezed again, four times in quick succession.

"That's what you're here to tell me? Hate to tell you, but he's dead... Don't you remember? Your husband killed him!"

Another sneeze. "Look, Morty wants you to know that he's ok with what happened. He knows it was an accident. He's at peace and he wants you to be also."

"He's ok with it? And just how would you know this?" She looked over her shoulder into the hallway then back at me again.

"Well, because Sal told me he is."

"Sal's dead! Both of you, harbingers of death!! Get back—get back!" She hooked her first finger of each hand into horns and spit between them. What she spewed landed on my shoe, which was infinitely better than what happened at the winery, but still grossed me out.

I sneezed again. "This is ridiculous. What the hell is going on?"

"Allergies maybe?" said Marley.

"Oh shit!" Sal started laughing. *"Remember, Babe, when we found out you had that latex allergy? I'll bet if you looked..."*

It took me a second, but I got it. "Latex? Oh! Awwwww gee, well, I'm not looking at anything!" I pulled up from a deep repressed part of my subconscious the hospital visit where an extremely good looking emergency intern needed to cut the "one size fits most" latex cat suit completely from my body as I swelled and sneezed simultaneously.

"Whatever you do, don't touch Mrs. Mitzner!"

"What did you say?" asked Mrs. Mitzner.

"Latex! You've got latex! Where is it? Back away, Mrs. Mitzner!" Another sneeze. I started panicking and thought my throat might close.

"Who? Me?" She wrapped her robe more tightly around her body. "Latex? You're crazy." I sneezed again.

Marley had put two and two together and, judging from her complexion, was on the verge of vomiting.

"Listen you have to hurry up and leave." Mrs. Mitzner looked again to the door.

I could hear footsteps coming down the stairs toward the front entrance. A vaguely familiar voice rang out "Hey, Sadie, you coming? On second thought, don't come without me! Hahahaha!"

Mrs. Mitzner leaned close to us and whispered "Rich doesn't know I was married…he thinks I'm still a virgin. Please don't blow it for me!"

"He thinks you're a what?" I sneezed again and thought my brain was going to explode. Sal was hysterical laughing in the background somewhere.

A middle-aged man wearing a loosely tied robe appeared in the doorframe. A gap revealed what I believed to be black latex underwear. He was about to open the screen door when we recognized each other.

His mouth dropped open and his hand reached behind him, searching for something to lean on as he stumbled back to the wall behind him.

"April! What are you doing here?"

I took a step and moved closer to him, my nose almost touching the screen door as I watched the color drain from his face. "You wouldn't want me to ask you that, would you Rich? What's the matter, things slow at the butcher's these days? "

"You stay away you, you...freak!"

I sneezed, and then sneezed again.

"I'm the freak? Who's wearing the latex undies, here?" I sneezed a third time but the last one was mainly for effect. I aimed it directly through the screen into the foyer.

"Ack!" He shrieked, jumped up, grappled for a car key from a hook on the wall and ran in the opposite direction of me, through the house. I heard the back door slam.

Mrs. Mitzner was just starting to figure out what was going on. We watched Rich run along the side of the house, to the street and jump into his Buick LeSabre. The tires left smoke and squealed as he backed out of the driveway.

"No, no, Rich, come back!" Mrs. Mitzner was running down the road, waving frantically with one hand and holding her robe together with the other.

The rear window of his car became just a dot in the distance. Realizing she wasn't going to catch up, Sadie Mitzner turned around and headed to the house. Her robe was now partially open, confirming the reason for my sneezing fits. I felt a little bad for her. All that latex and no one to scare with it.

She was giving me the evil eye as she walked up the porch, pointing. "April Serao, How could you?"

Marley intercepted. "Listen," she said "Your husband wanted us to give you a message. You need to see a doctor. There's something wrong with your heart."

I knew it was good to bring Marley along. I default to my right brain and she cattle prods my left.

Mrs. Mitzner said, "You two not only ruin the youngest action I've seen in years but you're nuts! You expect me to believe that?" She turned to the door.

Frantically, before she could get in the house, I yelled, "Morty said to remind you of the time you… well, the time you were on the roof of the garage."

She swung around to face me. "Huh? He said what?"

"That you guys did the nasty on the roof. He said you'd understand."

"Oh! That was the night we played 'Daydream Believer' over and over on the eight-track player. I love The Monkees. You know, I married Morty because he reminded me a little of Mike Nesmith, shorter of course, but he had the same eyes."

"Nesmith?? No way. Maybe Tiny Tim but I don't think Nesmith at all," said Marley.

"….Anyway, like I said Mrs. Mitzner, Sal sent me a message from Mr. Mitzner for you, that you need to have your heart checked. He says something isn't right."

She stared right through me.

"He still cares." Then she added, "What do you think heaven is like?"

Marley said, "I like to believe it's a place that you get to do all the things that make you happy. Eat chocolate, read, take bubble baths."

"That sounds nice. She was thoughtful for a moment. "Wait a minute. My Morty was happy playing cards. Hey, you don't think they play poker up there, do you? He knows I hate when he plays cards. I can't believe he'd be doing that." She took a breath. "Ok, I'll go to the doctor. Just go now, ok?"

"Morty doesn't believe she's gonna go."

"Thanks, Mrs. Mitzner." I said. "I am sorry about all of this. Listen, here's my number." I pulled out an old envelope from my purse and wrote it down with eyeliner, as I haven't had a pen in my purse since Chris was two months old. "Call me after you get it checked out and let me know what he says. I'd like to get the message to Morty, ok? He wants to know you're going to be all right."

"Thanks, Babe."

"You're welcome." I realized after I said it that I was talking out loud to a ghost.

It was funny, I was getting used to him being part of the conversation. It didn't throw me any longer and since it didn't, I responded to him like I would anyone else. Eventually, people were going to think I was certifiable if I didn't stop it, though.

Mrs. Mitzner nodded, oblivious to the fact that I was speaking to my husband who probably was throwing his share of an ante with Mr. Mitzner into a poker game pot as we spoke.

"Okay," she said, then glanced down the road with one last little wistful look. She wrapped her robe tight around her body and went into the house. I made a mental note to ask Sal if we could cross off another good deed.

Marley and I got in the car. "I feel like I just killed a puppy."

"You mean Mrs. Mitzner? You're kidding me right?" I looked at her incredulously. "That puppy is about three hundred and ninety eight in dog years and shrink-wrapped in latex. Get a visual going."

"Ok, I'm over it." She inspected the travel mug she'd left in the console of my car. Listen, we need to do a coffee run."

I agreed. I knew my caffeine levels were low because I hadn't gone to the bathroom for 45 minutes. It was time to step up the game. I needed the exercise.

I figure I kept in shape by doing my requisite two miles a day in bathroom sprints.

I was terrified to think what I'd look like if I skipped the potty circuit.

There was a Donut Dippers coffee shop not too far from my house so I kicked the Mini into gear and we headed that way. Marley flipped down the mirror and pulled out her tweezers. She was insanely fast when she was looking. Fur was flying in a matter of seconds and it was all I could do to keep from being buried under chin hair. As we pulled into the parking lot, I saw a red Nissan Altima. I checked the license plate: Y I AUTA. Yep. It was Chris's.

Marley and I went in and he was sitting at a booth sucking iced coffee through a straw.

"Heya, Chris," Marley said. "It's a sad, sad thing to see a man drinking alone."

Chris choked, paled and said "Oh, umm, hey Marley." He looked behind him, directly over his shoulder. As his head came back around he noticed me and he turned white. "Oh, hi Mom."

"Hey, kiddo." I noted the second iced coffee on the table. "So Chris, isn't there some sort of rule about barista's frequenting the coffee houses of competitors?"

"Yeah, like seven years bad luck or something," said Marley.

"Not when your boss is two tables over." He tilted his head to the right when he said it.

"Hey," I said. "Why are you drinking for two? Anything we should know about? You here with a friend?"

He turned and looked over his shoulder again. This time I noted that the bathrooms were that way. On a hunch I said, "Marley, keep Chris company for a minute and grab me a medium light latte please." I handed her a five-dollar bill. "I need to use the ladies room."

Chris twitched like someone had stuck a cattle prod up his ass. He grabbed my arm. "Ma, uhhh, can't you just get your coffee and use the bathroom at home? I'm sure it's a lot cleaner." He looked a lot like he did when he was four and I made him apologize to the owner of the local hardware shop for clipping a 23-cent plastic bracelet. If I recall, he had that same face right before he pooped his pants.

"I share a bathroom with three guys, remember? I just don't scare as easily as I used to. Be right back." As I walked to the bathroom, I gave a 'thumbs up' to the woman at the table Chris had nodded to. I pushed open the door and entered a small space painted an unfortunate shade of yellow, with two stalls, two sinks, and a large photograph of a chocolate cruller—also an unfortunate choice. One stall was free, the other taken. I looked under the closed stall door and saw a tan pair of feet with pink nail polish and a toe thong. Gillian.

I leaned against the sink and waited. And waited. Finally, from behind the door, a small voice said "C'mon, Mrs. Serao, how long are you going to stand there?"

"Well, hon, I've given birth to three kids and a caffeinated latte is on its way to me. I could spend the better part of the next two weeks in the bathroom."

The stall door opened.

"Hello, kiddo. Glad you came out." I said.

"I was risking my butt becoming one with the toilet."

The bathroom door flung open and Marley charged in. "Oh, there you are! You've been in here so long, I was about to toss you a flotation device. Hey, I'm worried about Chris. He's slightly green and hyperventilating in the booth. Oh, and your coffee's getting cold."

"Marley meet Gillian, Jack's daughter. Gillian, this is Marley, my friend and co-worker."

"Gillian? Ohhhh, as in Chris and Gillian. Does her father know she's here?"

"I don't know the answer to that, but I can take an educated guess. Ok, Gillian. C'mon. Follow me." We filed out of the bathroom and went to the table where Chris was waiting. Gillian slipped in next to him. Marley and I sat across from them.

"Gillian, I'm sure your father didn't bless your little boat ride over here. Where does he think you are?"

"Sleeping over a friend's house."

"Oh, well, this is going to go over well. Wait 'til he finds out your sleepover is with Chris. You need to call him."

Gillian looked at me as though I had just told her to go stick a fork in her eye. "Look, Mrs. Serao, if I catch the next ferry back to Connecticut, I'll be home in time for dinner. He doesn't need to know."

I gave a little smile. This stunt reminded me of my own younger days, not that I'd admit it. "Oh, no, my dear," I said. "That's not the way it works. You can call him, or I will. Take your pick."

"Ok, then, you do it." She tried to stare me down, but I gave her the Italian mommy look, which usually works best with a Bible in one hand and a wooden spoon held at ready in the other. Gillian gave a resigned sigh. "All right, I get it. I'll do it." Opening her cell phone, she hit a number on speed dial. A few seconds later she said, "Heya, dad. Well, actually a funny thing happened on the way to Amanda's. I kind of got detoured. Well, I'm not quite sure how it happened, but ummm, I'm on Long Island. Kind of at Chris's house. Well, not kind of, I am there...here whatever. Umm, yeah dad, April's Chris." She visibly cringed, waiting for the onslaught, and she wasn't disappointed.

We could all now clearly hear his end of the conversation. "How could you? I trusted you. You're grounded until you're out of the convent." I had to laugh at that one. "Let me talk to April please."

Gillian handed me the phone.

"Hey, Jack."

"April, hi." I heard him sigh. It reminded me of the sound he made as he was kissing my neck. I shuddered and felt a twinge of sadness. "I'm on my way to come get Gillian. Can you please keep her from doing anything else she shouldn't until I get there?" I weighed whether that was an effort at rapprochement with me, and decidedly probably not. I was a convenient stand in for Mother Superior, but still the crazy lady who talked to dead guys.

"No problem. Should we meet you at the ferry?"

"It's going to be a few hours, so you might as well go home. Take her with you. I'll head there, ok?" Maybe I was wrong.

"No problem," I said, trying to sound nonchalant. "Might as well have dinner while you're here—it will be about that time."

Jack's voice got lower, huskier, sexy. "I'd much prefer dessert, but, oh yeah, we aren't seeing each other. Bummer. Oh well, see you in a bit."

"No problem." I was sure I was blushing as I closed the phone and gave it back to Gillian. "Ok, kiddo, this is the deal. Your father is on his way to come get you. I'm responsible for you until the handoff happens, so let's go."

"Is it ok for Gillian to ride in my car?" asked Chris.

I hesitated. Rule number two in the childrearing manual clearly states "Never let them see you hesitate." Rule number one, of course, is "Always stand downwind so they don't smell your fear." My bad.

Marley filled the void, "Of course! April, they'll be fine."

"Ok, but you stay right in front of us. And keep your hands on top of your heads so I can see them."

"Uhhhh, mom, that'll be hard to do while I'm driving."

"I'll ride along and keep an eye on them."

"For some reason that doesn't make me feel any better."

"Huh?" said Chris.

"Nothing. C'mon. Let's go."

Marley and I got into the Mini. Traffic on Route 32 was moderate at this hour, with just the usual midday traffic as people pulled in and out of the shopping plazas and turned off onto side roads that led to pockets of small neighborhoods launched by various developers. I pulled out of the parking lot following Chris's car. Gillian stuck both her hands out of the passenger side window and flipped them over, then gave a thumbs up to assure us, I guess, that she wasn't touching anything she wasn't supposed to. Marley laughed and I decided that the kid was ok in my book.

We were taking a leisurely pace through lights and congestion when movement in my rearview mirror caught my eye. I turned my head quickly and saw Big Bird on steroids gaining on me. It turned out to be a canary yellow PT Cruiser about to take a bite out of my tail.

I couldn't go any faster because for the first time in recorded history, my son was doing the speed limit.

"Marley! Brace yourself!" I yelled. I got that awful sinking feeling when you know something unavoidable and bad is going to happen. I also thought about what Sal had said. Was this someone out to get me? A gangland-style hit? The car rammed us from behind. A great flash of yellow filled my brain as my head hit the windshield. The Mini lurched forward with a sickening crunch as my beloved car was crushed. I cut the wheel hard to the right so I would end up on the shoulder and not in Chris's trunk, while the Cruiser swerved left and collided with a stately oak tree on the other side of the road. The Mini came to a stop and I willed my hands to stop shaking. I looked over to my right. "Marley, are you ok?"

"I think so." She ran her hands over her thighs, her face, her arms. "Yeah, I think I'm fine. Just a little freaked. Oh, man April, your head. It's bleeding."

I touched my forehead and my hand came away red. The rearview mirror confirmed that I was indeed bleeding, but it didn't look too bad.

"What the hell happened?" Marley started searching the seat and the floor with her hands.

"I'm not exactly sure, but I'm about to find out!"

"I'll be with you in a minute. I seem to have lost my tweezers."

I took off my seatbelt and got out of the car. "Unbelievable!" I started storming across the road yelling at the other driver. "What the hell were you thinking?"

"Uh, oh April. I think the guy might be having a heart attack."

"What do you mean? Sal, aren't you supposed to give me a heads up on these things? And was he *trying* to hit me? You have me looking over my shoulder for some whack job with a knife and duct tape."

"This one isn't on the agenda, Babe. So I guess, yeah, he could have been. Did you get a dog yet?"

Chris had stopped his car, flung open the door and started racing back to me. "Ma! Your head!"

I yelled back. "I'm fine, just call the police." They huddled around the Mini, unintentionally but thankfully obscuring the damage, and while Chris spoke urgently into his cell phone, I ran to the other car. Marley apparently had found her tweezers because she was right behind me.

A dark-haired driver with a classic Fifties ducktail and long sideburns slumped over the steering wheel. I opened the door and gingerly pushed him back against the seat. He wore no shirt under his white suit jacket, which was unbuttoned to his waist. Both the jacket and the skintight pants were finished off with silver edging.

"Marley! Looks like we have Elvis here."

Marley's head popped in through the passenger side window. "Oh, my God! I've had a recurring fantasy for twenty years or so that's a lot like this. Is he unconscious? Because if so, this is my fantasy and you have to leave."

We had been traveling at about thirty miles an hour, so the driver could have been hurt from the impact, but he was wearing his seatbelt and he didn't look bruised anywhere.

I would have to get him to a hard surface if I needed to administer chest compressions, but I didn't think it was a good idea to move him unless I had to, so I poked him a time or two to see if he was breathing.

"Mister. Hey mister, are you ok?" No response.

Sal appeared next to me wearing a white toga and had a grape leaf crown covering a good portion of the bald. *"Oh no! It's Elvis! Hey man, you ok?"* he asked. Still no response. *"I don't think he's breathing. Elvis! You ok?"*

"Sal, c'mon. Do you think this guy can hear you? And don't they have pants in heaven? This cross-dressing thing has me concerned."

"April, do you think you're talking to Sal? Sal in a dress? You must have hit your head hard." Shoot. I had forgotten about Marley.

"Well, no, he probably can't hear me. I forget sometimes what reality I'm in. But he's not breathing right? Because administering CPR to a breathing patient is not advisable."

"Well if that Smurf color he's turning is any indication, I'd have to say he's not breathing." Big Birds, Smurfs, and The King. It was all like a twisted reality show.

Marley said, "Oh, just give him a wet willy. That'll fix him right up."

"What?"

"You know, a wet willy. My uncle used to do it to me all the time.'

"Marley, I don't think I need to know this."

"Oh, for Pete's sake, April." She stuck her index finger into her mouth and swirled her tongue around it. She pulled it out, still dripping, and showed it to me.

"Ok, that's DISGUSTING!"

"Make way, 'cause here it comes! It's wet willy time!" She took the finger and shoved it into Elvis's ear, wiggled it around a few times for good measure, then pulled it out. It made a slight popping sound.

The driver's body stiffened, board-like, for a moment. Then he took a huge gasping breath and began flailing wildly with his hands, his eyes opened wide, terrified. They were a perfect shade of blue. He was a dead ringer for Elvis.

"Wow, Marley, this guy is a great an imposter. He totally looks like Elvis."

"That's 'cause I'm pretty sure it is Elvis, babe."

Before I could answer, emergency services pulled up; one ambulance and five cop cars. Three people climbed out of the back of the ambulance and ran to the Cruiser while Marley and I moved away to give them room to work. One of the rescuers was my neighbor, Reese, who I almost didn't recognize in her full EMT gear.

The EMTs stabilized the driver, and Reese broke away from the others as they loaded him into the ambulance and came over to us, followed by two police officers.

"Hey, Reese."

"Hey! April. Leave it to you to wrangle with Elvis." She laughed. "Are you ok? Your friend there? You need me to check you out?" I shook my head. Reese stared at the bump above my left eyebrow that was causing my head to throb. "I think we need to look at that."

The officer to her left spoke. "Ma'am, my name is Officer Anthony Perrone, and this here is my partner, Officer Clancy. What happened here?"

Reese gestured to me. "Guys, this is April, my neighbor."

Tony's eyes opened wide. "April? You know, funny thing, you look a lot like a lady who's house I was called to a few years ago. April Serao. Her husband died while…well, while…" he began to look a little grey.

Oh, for goodness sake. I helped him out. "Having sex. Yeah I know all about it. I'm that April."

Without taking his eyes off me, Officer Perrone put his hand on Clancy's shoulder and propelled both of them backwards. "Uhhh, we're going to talk to the others." He did a head nod toward Chris and Gillian, then both turned and ran.

Sal was hysterical laughing in the background. *"That shit just never gets old."*

Death Is A Relative Thing

Chapter 11

"Death's gang is bigger and tougher than anyone else's.
Always has been and always will be. Death's the man."
— Michael Marshall, The Upright Man

As mighty as I believed my Mini to be, it lost in the PT
Cruiser battle. It was too damaged to drive so a tow truck had been
dispatched. I didn't want to stick around to watch the removal. I
lost the battle with Reese. She bandaged my head mummy-style
and gave me strict instructions on what to do if I felt sick, started
seeing double, or thought I was Lindsay Lohan or something. I
didn't ask her what I should do if I started having conversations
with my dead husband. We were told we could go home, but
to expect an officer to stop by to get an official statement since
Perrone and Clancy had left the party early. Marley and I got into
Chris's car and we drove the few miles to my house.

"Marley, did that guy—you know, the driver of the other car—look familiar to you?"

"Yeah, well, *duh*. Elvis."

"Not what I meant. He obviously can't be Elvis. I'm wondering who he might really be. He certainly looked familiar."

"April, babe, he looked familiar because he is Elvis."

"Not now." Damn! I kept forgetting not to talk to Sal out loud.

"April?" She shrugged off my indiscretion and thought for a moment. "Ditch the wig and he'd look a bit like the guy that popped out of the cake at my grandmother's 94th birthday party, remember? You were there."

"The guy with the cowboy hat, guns, and G-string chaps? Nah, I don't remember him at all."

Marley laughed. "The party company certainly screwed up. Oh well, my grandmother had a great time."

"Yeah, she did. For a lady on a pension, she a lot of one-dollar bills in her purse that just kept on pulling out and waving in the air."

Marley was thoughtful for a second. "I bet I could I.D. the guy from the waist down, though I liked him better as The King. You think there's a chance they would leave his suit jacket on but remove his pants so I could check him out?"

We made the right onto my street to find it cordoned off by an officer, a black-and-white police cruiser, and two sawhorses. Chris slammed on his brakes.

He stuck his head out the window and spoke to the officer. "What's going on?"

"TV cameras and vans are blocking the road. You can't go down here now," the cop said.

"But we live here! We need to go down the street."

"Which house?"

"Number 22, the cape with the dead plants and the rusted bike on the porch."

"Oh…*that* house. Well then, why didn't you say?" He chuckled and stepped to the side, moving one of the sawhorses over to give us access. "Good luck!"

We navigated an obstacle course of cars, vans, and milling crowds. I glanced at Helen Krupshaw's house and noted that she had pulled her chair to the middle of her lawn for a better view of the show. I don't know how she knew I was in Chris's car, but as we passed, she glared straight into the back seat, pushed out her right fist, turned it over and gave me the finger. I didn't have much time to reflect on it, though, distracted as I was by my front lawn.

"Uh, Ma, what am I supposed to do?" Chris stopped the car. The property looked like a giant active Petri dish culture. Reporters were crawling over each other for better position. "The neighbors are all gawking…and look, there's a hot dog kiosk in the driveway."

"That reminds me, I'm hungry," said Marley. "Think he's got Italian ice over there? Sometimes they do you know. Lemon used to be my favorite but now they have piña colada and I swear I get a buzz off it." She started to open the door to get out of the car.

"Well the neighbors are watching the show, all right. Either that or all the dogs in the neighborhood needed to be walked at the same time," Gillian said. "Can you grab me a rainbow ice while you're at it? Wait, is that a cotton candy machine by the azalea bush? "

"Marley, what the heck are you doing? Get back in here," I said, peering deeper into the crowd. A camera crew had set up lights right smack in the middle of my one and only rose bush. I spotted my son.

"I think I see Brian over there." He looked confused and sweaty, his glazed eyes searching past the phalanx of reporters with hand-held microphones surrounding him. He spotted Chris's car and mouthed "Help me, please." I scanned the yard for Scott and found him a few feet behind Brian, pinned down by three reporters and as many cameras, backed up against the porch with no way to escape. I went directly into *Mommy, save me!* mode.

"Ok, everyone, listen to me. We have to stay together. I'll get out first." I pushed myself from the car, grabbed Gillian's hand, told Chris to grab hers, and had Marley play caboose. "Don't let go no matter what happens. We have to stick together!" My eyes never left Brian. I reflected for a second, and switched mental gears into Suburban Mall Christmas Shopping mode. I snaked the group in and out among reporters and crew, elbowing and/or tripping them when necessary. As we neared our target, I let out a war whoop.

"AAAAHWEEEEEEEEHHHHHHHHHHHH!"

The camera crew jumped back, surprised, which gave me an opportunity to intercept. With my free hand I grabbed Brian's arm and pulled him out of the melee. I gave him a shove toward daylight. "Run, Brian, run!" I did a quick zig and yelled for Chris to grab Scott. When he made contact, I zagged. Everything moved in slow motion—the swath we cut in the throng with our body chain, my sons' rescue—and it was surreal but effective, the six of us, a veritable human chainsaw cutting through the crowd.

I was panting and drenched in sweat by the time we got to the front door and tried to collapse inside. It was locked. I did a quick reach-around for my purse and felt only air. I had left my purse in the car. My car. The Mini.

My purse held my house keys, makeup, wallet, and every last cent I had.

"Brian, give me your keys."

He shook his head. "Left them home."

"Scott?"

"No, Ma'am. I figured I'd just push Brian through the front window like we usually do." His eyes nervously panned the crowd. "We may still have to go that route."

The reporters were gaining on us. They were only a few feet away and asking questions, shoving microphones in our faces. The kids were working on the window. I heard it open and glanced behind me in time to see Brian's feet being shoved through it. Chris and Gillian were pinned up against the door behind me; Marley and I stood in front, guarding. A video camera filmed from the corner of the porch. Our escape was not going as smoothly as I had planned.

Brian opened the door from the inside and the other kids fell through it, and Marley and I quickly piled in. I slammed and locked the door behind us and we wound our way into the kitchen, the furthest room from the mob.

"Damn, I forgot to get my hot dog. You think I can run out real qui—" I looked over at her and Marley was smart enough not to finish the sentence.

"Ma, how do you get into these things? It's all over the news that you got into a car accident with Elvis Presley."

"What? C'mon Scott, he's been dead forever. It was obviously an impersonator. Why is everyone making such a big deal about it?" I thought back to the perfect blue eyes and the made-to-fit suit. Could it have been like Sal said? "He did resemble Elvis, but there's no way Marley's wet willy resuscitated a dead man."

"Marley gave Elvis a wet willy? You've got to be kidding!" Gillian was clearly having a good time, which I don't think was the ultimate point in having her wait for her father with me.

"You are just uninformed, April." Marley sat up a little straighter in her chair, pointed at me and said. "I've delivered a good many wet willies in my day, and let me tell you, they are very effective."

"Well, April, I think he may very well have been Elvis. The Elvis. He's done this type of thing before. I checked around, and no one here has seen him since yesterday morning."

Damn! Sal and I needed to talk, but finding quiet time alone with him was just as hard now as it had been six years ago when the kids were younger.

I edged my way out of the kitchen into the bathroom, locked the door and leaned against the sink. "Sal! Sal!" Hopefully I kept it low enough that the crew in the next room over couldn't hear me—and low enough that the reporters' mikes couldn't pick it up—but loud enough to sound urgent. "Sal!"

"*Hey, Babe.*" He appeared in front of me wearing overalls and a jacket. He held a pitchfork.

"What is this now? Are you posing for an *American Gothic* revival?"

"*Nah. Today we had a practice. I'm in the reserves and once a month we have training, just in case...well...*" Sal lowered his voice. "*In case the Other Side ever mounts an attack. We don't expect to ever have to make real use of any of these exercises, but I know a lot of angels who are happy we're looking out for them.*"

"Female angels, I'm sure, right Sal? Anyway, wasn't that battle fought like a million years ago?"

"*Don't know. My knowledge of history is pretty much limited to post-1950.*"

"Well, I'd be a little concerned if I were you. Think about it, Sal. They gave you a pitchfork, but they won't give you a halo? Doesn't that seem just a little counterintuitive to you?"

Sal cocked his head and looked at me, obviously confused.

I tried to clarify. "Maybe they are preparing you for the worst, like you just may not cut it and need to be, well, sent down under."

"*April, heaven isn't some schoolroom you can get expelled from!*"

"I don't know Sal. I think there's been some sort of precedent set, and you might want to read up on that. Anyway, none of it matters right this second. You said the real Elvis might have been driving the PT Cruiser that hit me. What did you mean by that?"

"*Oh, yeah. Elvis has a way of sneaking past the gatehouse now and again. Right now the Pearly Gates are being painted,*" *some urban renewal thing. Anyway, this angel, her name's Penny, like as in, Pennies from Heaven, get it?"*

"Yeah, Sal, I got it…the point is?"

"Well, the point is, she's real new up here and first thing she does is put a note in the suggestion box that the Pearly Gates are too plain, not pearly enough. Boring even. So the Big Guy sets her up painting flowers and vines—you know, beautification."

"She's new and gets to do that? Betcha she's not on a restricted halo."

"Focus, April. Anyway, seems she didn't know that Elvis splits occasionally, and my understanding is that he was able to sweet talk his way past her. I've been trying to gather some info. Stuff like this isn't exactly broadcast."

"Wow, they let a new angel paint the Pearly Gates? She must have some pull. Sal, have they ever let you paint anything? Forget I asked. I assume they know all about our kitchen. Hey, why can I touch Elvis? You can't be felt or move things. How can he drive? If he was an angel, wouldn't he be…well, like you?"

"April, I am following the rules and protocol. If that person is The King, remember, he is here without approval; therefore, it's open season for him. Me, I'm playing by the rules."

"So what you're telling me is that if you had just been your normal self and not been so damned politically correct, I could have gotten a hug or, better yet, we could be having wild and crazy sex right now? I mean, I couldn't kill you twice right? Somehow this all doesn't seem quite fair."

"Mom? Mom, you ok in there?" Scott gave few quick raps to the bathroom door. "Who are you talking to?"

"Hold on a sec! I'll be right there."

"I know it's not fair, April, and I'm sorry. You have no idea. Listen, I have to get back. My unit needs me—they're a pitchfork short right now. Someone's gotta keep heaven safe for eternity and all that."

"Yeah Sal. You'll let me know if Elvis did indeed decide to leave the building, ok?'

"Ok, Babe, you got it. I'll get back to you with my findings." He did a high sign under his chin and as he faded from view. I could swear I got a quick whiff of hay and heard a cow moo off in the distance.

I flushed the toilet and ran the water in the sink just in case anyone was listening. Then I made my way back to the kitchen.

"They're still there! On our lawn!" Brian jogged in from the living room, having gone on a reconnaissance run. His eyes looked twice as large as normal and he was drenched in sweat.

The situation was untenable. Someone needed to take a stand. Oh, well. My house, my platform.

"I've had just about enough of this. Marley, watch the kids. I'm going out there."

"Well, you can't go like that, thrown to the wolves, unprotected." Marley sized me up, opened my pot drawer, grabbed the colander and put it on my head.

Chris fished for the huge saucepot lid and handed it to me. "Use it as a shield," he said. I started to protest but before I could speak, two shish kebab skewers were stuffed into my free hand. Scott ripped a length of aluminum foil off the roll and began to wrap my arms.

"What are you guys, nuts? I'm not wearing this stuff!" I turned around, ripping at the foil, and found Jack standing right in front of me. I snatched at my head in an attempt to remove the colander but only managed to push it over to one side.

"Well, well. You look like a cross between the Tin Man and King Tut. But of course, your legs are much nicer than either of theirs." I had forgotten about my bandaged head. I guess I looked surprised to see him, because he added, "Sorry, I knocked and there wasn't an answer. There are desperate people surrounding the porch, so I let myself in. Hope you don't mind, April."

He looked good. Great, in fact. His hair was disheveled and he was dressed in jeans and a lightweight black tee. His eyes trolled down my body and back up again. I was enjoying the ogle, but I was distracted by a rustle behind me and heavy breathing on the back of my neck.

Sigh. Without turning around I knew who it was. "Jack, let me introduce my friend Marley. Marley, meet Jack. Now can I get back to this? I have to get these people out of here. I need to confront them."

"So, that's the plan? You were headed out the front door…in that?"

"Yeah, I was jus…"

"Ok, wait a second, stay right there." Jack opened the drawer under the oven and took out a cookie sheet. He shifted me to face him, making sure my back was to everyone else in the kitchen. Then he lifted my tee shirt a bit and stuffed the pan underneath it running his hands softly down the side of my body. His warmth was delicious and it spread quickly south. Pulling my shirt down over the baking sheet, he smiled and said, "Better! You can't be too careful, April. It's vicious out there."

"AAARRRGGGHH! You guys are all crazy." I didn't take any of it off, though. Sal's words, *They're gunning for you*, reverberated in my head. I made my way to the foyer.

Marley followed me and everyone else followed her. She stopped when I got to the front door and turned to address the room.

"Attention, everyone! As we all know, our beloved April is going out regain her land and restore order. Be forewarned... She may be tortured. She may yell and possibly cry. She may bang on the door and beg for us to let her back in, but we must stand tall and remain united. Do not, I repeat, do *not* open the door until her mission is complete. Stay the course."

"Huh? What are you insane? Marley, you just totally screwed up any possibility of getting an Italian ice on my watch." I took one last look at my house, my children, and my friends, took a deep breath, gave thumbs up, turned and pushed my way through the door.

The moment I hit the porch, they descended like locusts on a field of wheat.

A young female reporter got to me first. "How do you feel knowing you almost killed Elvis Presley?"

"Huh? No, no, that's not what happened. First of all, he hit me. Second, he's can't be the real Elvis. Elvis is already dead—that's not something many people recover from."

"Right, but how did you feel knowing you could have killed The King?" She smiled earnestly and I grimaced back.

"Are you old enough to even remember Elvis Presley? Look, is there anyone out there with a legitimate question?"

A more mature-looking gentleman in a suit and round glasses approached me with a microphone. "I'd just like to ask one quick question. How do you feel, knowing you could have killed Elvis Presley?"

I grabbed the microphone from his hands and shouted into it, "I did not hit Elvis Presley's car. He hit mine. Additionally, The King is dead. It was obviously an actor, an impersonator, in the other vehicle."

I heard the truck before I saw it. Suddenly there was a commotion near the street and I heard her voice rise above the throng. "Cease this right now! Who are you crazy people? Get the hell out of my way." The crowd started parting like the waters of the red sea.

My mother appeared from nowhere and created a pathway few dared to follow, forged with a loud mouth, ethnic hand gestures, and Cherry Cola Red #17 hair (aisle ten of *Libbet's Drugs*). She climbed the porch and eyed me up and down. "April, I sure hope *this* getup doesn't make the front cover of *News Long Island*."

One reporter slipped behind my mother and made the mistake of bumping lightly into her. My mother turned, stared down her nose at the reporter, then did the Italian *malocchio* thing, making the evil eye with her hands.

A hush fell on the crowd and some members of the reporter's crew actually looked like they were going to cry. My mother surveyed the crowd, taking her time, making sure she pierced everyone on the lawn with her gaze.

The first reporter started moving briskly away from me. Within moments, that scene had repeated itself numerous times with all the news reporters and camera people. It was as if they all had a "collective consciousness" as they began packing up en masse, a bit frenzied, moving quickly, almost racing to get off my lawn and into their vehicles. The local news van left a streak of rubber and smoke on the street in an attempt to escape. In the space of seven minutes, my had mother managed to clear the yard. Even old Krupshaw went inside.

"Oh, April, why do you always make things harder than they need be?"

I surveyed the wreckage from my porch. Empty water bottles and coffee cups were strewn everywhere. My rose bush was bent and the lawn, a thriving crop of crabgrass, was trampled, and stuck to itself. I heard the screen door creak open and everyone from the house joined us on the porch.

The only person left on the property was the hot dog vendor, who I now recognized as Hot Dog Eddie. He looked around, confused. Eddie usually situated his hot dog kiosk on the shoulder of Highway 25 between the florist and the shooting range. He's a short man with an Italian accent, in his seventies, sporting a shock of white hair. Very handsome in his youth, he was still attractive even now. As long as I've known him, I've never seen him without a signature Robusto cigar hanging off the side of his mouth or without Paola the mechanical talking parrot, which hung suspended from the umbrella attached to his cart.

I turned to the crew on the porch. "Stay here for a minute." It didn't take me long to reach Eddie.

"Heya, Eddie. You ok?" The eyes that were moments earlier sparkling as he chatted up the ladies and talked trash sports with the men were now flat and sported a tiny tear as he peered into a steamer full of unsold Sabretts with a pile of warm buns off to the side. He'd been running a very brisk business.

"Hi, April. Sorry about your lawn and all." He wiped at his face with his sleeve.

"It's ok. We never could grow any real grass here anyway."

"Oh, and I guess that's my fault too right?"

"Hey baby, nice ass!" said the parrot.

"Eddie, are you ever going to teach that parrot to say anything else?"

"Nah, that works just fine for me."

I watched as the cigar moved from the left side of his mouth to the right. I wasn't sure how he did it because his lips never moved.

"Ya know, just for you April, because we've known each other so long and stuff, I'm gonna offer you my world famous, first-ever half and half sale starting right now. Everything here half price for the next half hour only. Whaddya say?" He hooked his thumbs under his red and white striped suspenders, looked at the crew on my porch and smiled broadly, all teeth and cigar, smoke encircling his head.

"Including the Italian ice?"

He hesitated, but bounced back quickly. "Yes, ma'am."

I stuck my hand out and he shook it solidly. "Sounds like you've got a deal." I turned around and yelled out, "Hey guys, dinner's done!"

Scott said, "I didn't hear the smoke alarm."

I ignored him and started handing out plates. We all ate hot dogs and chips on the front porch, Eddie included.

Jack and I sat together on one of the wide steps. Our shoulders touched occasionally and I felt the warmth surge through my body. I liked having him around but wasn't sure how long it was going to last. I mean, my circumstances hadn't changed any. I was still seeing, and talking to, dead people.

"Damn, April," said Sal. *"No onions? Really?"*

I put Sal on "ignore."

We had done some real damage to the hot dog surplus and had just started dishing out Italian ice cups when a black and white police car stopped in front of the house. Two officers got out and walked to the porch. Naturally, the force had sent women, apparently not wanting to take any chances.

"April Serao?"

"That's me."

"April, I don't know if you remember me, but we went to high school together. I'm Officer Babbit and this is Officer Jeffries. We need to ask you some questions about the accident this afternoon. Do you have a few minutes to discuss it?"

I had to think back, but I did remember her. Her name was Lea but we used to call her Babbit the Wabbit because she had this tendency to twitch her nose, and she looked forever like she walked in on a fart. I wouldn't have thought she'd go into law enforcement. The other officer was short and wide. 'Babbit and Costello' came to mind.

"But, Babe, c'mon. No onions?"

"Sure." Argh! Sal was killing me. I swung my arm around and offered them a seat on the steps. "So, did you two draw the short straws? None of the boys wanted to risk their lives coming out to see me, right?"

Babbit smiled and said, "Let's just say, they all remembered emergency proctology appointments when this assignment came up. By the way, we stopped to take a look in at the damage to your car and saw this inside." She opened the bag and pulled out my purse. "Figured you might need it."

"Oh, yeah, all my makeup is in there. Tomorrow could have been a very bad day. Thanks a lot."

"Really. Babe. Don't you remember, the onions are in that wonderful tomato sauce? Look, just go get one more hot dog, with onions please. I need it."

"ARGH!" I slapped myself on the forehead. "It's not like you have to deal with the heartburn or the calories! Stop!"

Jack slid away from me and shook his head. Officer Babbit studied my face, probably to determine whether I was high.

"Had you been drinking? Doing any sort of drugs? Were you under the influence when you ran into Elvis?"

"Oh, for Pete's sake. No! And I didn't run into Elvis…he ran into me!"

"Well, we have to ask. I mean, April, everyone saw the picture of you in *The End*. You know, the issue with the winery photo where that guy was on top of you. My goodness, you *had* to be drunk to let him go there."

Sal was hysterical in the background. Even Jack cracked a smile.

I explained the traffic accident to the officers without having to slam my head against anything to keep Sal out of it. Babbit handed me a business card.

"This is the auto body shop your car was towed to. You can move it to another if you like, but this is the one on call today."

I was glad I hadn't witnessed the towing of my poor Mini.

"Um, there's something else, April. When we went to check the damage to your car, the hood had been spray painted."

"Huh?"

"It says 'Watch your back BITCH.' "

My car! I was now hyperventilating. "Does it wipe off?"

"No April, it's real spray paint. It's not coming off. Do you have any idea who could have done that?"

"What color?"

Officer Jeffries looked through her notes. "Metallic blue. The skull though, that's black. Kind of hard to see it from the angle it's at though"

Skull? My poor car. "Angle?"

"Uh, yeah, it's hanging."

"Huh? The skull was hanging?"

"Well, no, the *car* was hanging." Jeffries was looking at her notes again, possibly to keep from laughing. "From a noose, placed where the right headlight would have been."

"If, of course, it was still there," said Babbit.

"They could never have done that with a Hummer. I always told you bigger is better." Sal again.

"Pretty neat trick though, how they did it. Leverage and all that."

Babbit shot Jeffries a look. "Really, April, we need to know if you have any enemies or know who might have done it?"

Uh oh. In my mind I ran through different ways to tell that tale and decided there was no way to explain it without getting thrown into some long-term psych ward.

"No, Officers. I have no idea who would have done that."

Sigh. Tomorrow could *still* be a very bad day.

After I convinced them that I hadn't been drunk at the time of the mishap or anytime thereafter—but hoped to be very, very soon—the officers left, promising to keep me informed concerning the status of the case and the continuing health of the other dead man in my life recently, Elvis.

Chapter 12

"The easiest kind of relationship for me is with 10,000 people. The hardest is with one."

— **Joan Baez**

My mother and Hot Dog Eddie left at the same time, and Marley shortly afterwards. The boys and Gillian were playing video games and eating chips in the den while Jack and I sat on the glider in the back yard, each nursing a glass of White Zinfandel compliments of *Trefal Winery*. It was beautiful out, with a soft breeze helped to cool off the day's heat.

"It's getting late. I don't think the ferry runs after nine p.m. You'll never make it."

"I know. I was thinking about staying the night,"

"Whoa, Cowboy! Are you kidding me? April, I don't care if this yahoo is the poster boy for Microphallus Anonymous—he

ain't staying here! My house, my rules. There's a hotel off the expressway."

I let the comment slide.

Jack continued, "I saw a hotel off the expressway a few miles back. I'll call and see if they have any rooms available, but truly, that probably isn't going to make me worry any less."

"Better, although we could just let him swim to Connecticut. Don't worry, I'll spot him."

"Worry about what?"

"April, c'mon. Someone spray painted your car with a nasty-gram. They hung your car. Do you have any idea why that would have happened?"

"No, not a clue." I was a little nervous though. I was hoping Sal had been wrong. "If I could figure out how to make it work, you'd be more than welcome to stay here, but I'm short beds and rooms. There's always the floor...I think I have a few airbeds in the garage if that's ok."

I heard Sal choke.

Jack moved his body a little closer to mine and reached for my hand. "You know, I just had a thought. You and I could take the hotel room and leave the kids here." He smiled.

"Yup, great idea. I'm sure Chris, Brian, and Scott would be glad to have Gillian as an overnight guest. With no adult supervision."

"Good point."

"Yep. I've been doing this for a while."

"Ok, April, let's go see if we can find those airbeds. But first, about tomorrow. I'll make arrangements to drop Gillian off at the ferry in the morning and have her mom pick her up in Bridgeport. You and I can spend the day together, alone, maybe look for a guard dog. What do you say?"

"No on the dog and before I say yes to us being together, you need to know that I still hear Sal. Nothing has changed in the week we haven't seen each other."

"April, I didn't expect it would. What I did find, though, is that this week was long and lonely. I just know I want to be with you. As long as you feel the same way, we'll work out the details as we go along."

I nodded.

We shared a comfortable quiet, finished our wine and then found two airbeds in the garage. We began setting them up.

Chris put his controller down. "Oh, overnight guests?" He chanced a quick glance at Gillian.

"Yep." said Jack, "Gillian and I will be taking over here. Hope you don't mind."

"Nope, not at all. But you know," Chris continued, smiling broadly, "these airbeds can get a little uncomfortable, especially for someone, well, older. If you want Jack, I can let you sleep in my room. The mattress will be better for your back."

Jack laughed. "Nice try, Slick, but I don't think I'm so old that you're gonna get that one past me." He looked Gillian's way.

I felt like I was at the OK Corral standing between Wyatt Earp and Billy Clanton.

The cowboy stepped down first. "Hey, can't blame a guy for trying! Night guys." Chris turned to the stairs. Scott and Brian said good night and followed him.

I brought the chip bowl and soda glasses into the kitchen and deposited them into the sink. When I turned around, I found myself face to face with Jack.

He closed the gap between me and the sink, gently taking a piece of my hair and twirling it between his fingers. "You know," he said, reaching down with his lips to mine, "I might be able to sneak away for a little bit, maybe meet you, say, upstairs? Your room?"

His lips moved with purpose down my neck, then reached the top of my breasts. I held the back of his head, willing him to move down further, for his tongue to…

"April! April, baby! Just got word it WAS Elvis that hit your Mini. Absolutely without a doubt."

Oh boy. How was I ever going to handle this?

I spent the night alone and alert, listening for any sounds of Chris or Gillian roaming the house, as well as noose-wielding ninjas, so I begged off driving to the ferry and slept in. Jack was back at the house by ten a.m. with enough food to restock the kitchen. After putting away the groceries, he started cooking pancakes and bacon. I began to think this was a pretty decent arrangement and that he would have to be so under-endowed that he indented before this scenario became bad. Chris was already up, texting Gillian non-stop. The other boys were sleeping and, since it was Sunday, my expectation was that they would remain prone until at least noon. I was in the bedroom trying to find something to wear that didn't make me look overweight, pre-periodic and suspiciously like my grandmother. It didn't help that any moment I was going to be summoned downstairs for breakfast, preferably clothed, so I was under pressure. I was standing knee deep in a pile of clothes, wearing only my bra and underwear, when I was interrupted.

"So, Babe, did you get that guard dog yet?"

"No, Sal. I don't want a dog." I dug through the pile and located a pair of jeans that I had rejected just minutes before. "What I'd like more than anything is to occasionally get a few minutes of privacy while I dress." I put the pants on.

"Hey, you didn't have to lie on the bed to zip them! Way to go April. Did you lose weight?"

"Don't know. I haven't weighed myself in a long time. It's too time consuming."

"How much time can it take? The scale is right under the sink for goodness sake. You stand on it then read the number."

"Unfortunately, it's not that simple. Timing is everything. Scales are to be used only first thing in the morning before eating and after going to the bathroom. I have to shave my legs, brush my teeth, clip the nails on both my hands and feet and get my hair trimmed. The glasses come off and so do my rings. Then, and only then, can I get on a scale. Oh, and if it's between one and four weeks before my period, I take off five pounds for bloating."

Sal laughed. "Babe, the only thing you missed was donating an organ."

"That may be next."

"How about getting an attack llama? I hear they're pretty loyal—and they keep the grass trimmed."

"No, Sal."

"Guard geese?"

"Sal, I know you're worried, but I'm fine. I can take care of myself. Besides, nothing's happened and I doubt anything will."

"Sure, and the graphics on your car are a perverse love tap. Listen April, be careful. I can only do so much from where I am."

"Might I remind you that I only saved him because you told me to?"

"Yeah, and April, that's the strangest part about all this. I usually have pretty good instincts when it comes to people. I'd have sworn he was one of the good ones."

I heard Chris at the bottom of the stairs. "Ma, breakfast is ready!"

"Sal, I gotta go, but next time we talk we need to discuss where you get your info from.

Chris was at the table pouring orange juice into glasses while Jack stood at the counter buttering toast. The table was set for five and there was a pile of bacon in the middle. A large cast iron skillet filled with eggs and cheese sat off to the side next to a full pot of coffee. I hadn't realized how hungry I was until then.

"Jack, this is incredible."

"Yeah mom, it's called B-R-E-A-K-F-A-S-T. You know, that meal you disavow any knowledge of because you don't cook before noon?"

I used some effective parenting skills and ignored Chris. "Jack, wow, this is wonderful. I hate to disappoint you though. I see the table's set for five, but guaranteed Scott and Brian won't get up until lunchtime."

My children love to prove me wrong. Occasionally they do so with flawless timing, as they did then. My other two boys came barreling down the stairs. I watched as they hit the landing, skidded, and shot into the kitchen.

"Wow, it's breakfast!" said Brian.

Scott added, "Oh, mom, look the stove is being used before noon! See, there's no gypsy curse on it!"

I heard Sal laughing.

Scott reached across the table to grab a piece of bacon. "So mom, is it true that someone may be after you? That's what the cops said yesterday, right?"

"Yeah, but don't worry about it. I think it's all just a bad joke, although spray painting my car was certainly in poor taste."

"I don't know about that," said Jack. "April, you need to take this seriously. You really should get a dog."

"No dog!"

"Let's do it! A big dog!" said Brian.

"No dogs, period. They're like children, and I'm working on getting a few out of the house, not bringing in more."

"Nice, ma." Chris put down his juice and looked around. "Uh, does anyone else smell smoke?"

Force of habit caused me to look toward the stove, but it was fine. I mean, after all, I hadn't been cooking. I did smell smoke, however.

We all got up and scattered, looking. The smell got stronger in the foyer, but nothing was burning. Inside, anyway. I opened the front door.

A fire blazed in the center of the porch. It hadn't consumed the porch yet, but it wouldn't take long. Dead plants burn fast. Jack came up behind me.

"Shit, April. What the hell! Call 911."

"By the time they get here, the porch will be gone."

He stared through me for a second then raced to the kitchen yelling, "Boys, hurry! Grab some pots."

We set up a bucket brigade from Chris to Brian to Scott to me then Jack. In under 10 minutes the fire was out, and my living room carpet was soaked.

I stared at the charred, gaping hole between the front door and the porch stairs. "Looks like the back door is the new front door."

"April, what's going on? Who's doing this...and why?"

I already knew who, of course. First my car, now the house. "Jack, I can't tell you how I know, but I believe the winery toad is responsible for this. He's in a gang called the Fenders, so they're probably all in it together, but it doesn't make sense. If they're pissed I screwed up their hit against him, why not just shoot me? I mean, they defaced my car, of all things. Who ever heard of a passive-aggressive street gang?"

"It sounded like you just said 'hit' as in 'contract to kill' and 'gang' all in the same breath. We're going to get you a dog right now. Let me grab my keys." He walked toward the kitchen.

I yelled after him. "No dog. You think the boys are ok here? I'm not sure I should leave them"

"I'll watch over them, April. Go get a dog."

"No dog, Sal. And what are you going to do if there is any trouble?"

"Don't worry about it. I got friends. Nothing will happen."

"Surprisingly, I'm not the least bit comforted by that Sal."

I armed the boys with Officer Babbit's phone number, a can of mace, and the whistle that I kept on my keychain. "Don't open the door, don't answer the phone unless it's me, and don't stand near any windows. Got it?"

Brian said, "You're kidding, right?"

"No not at all. Remember those child harnesses I hooked you guys up to when you were babies? I'm prepared to pull them from the attic and take you with us if necessary. The choice is yours."

Thirty minutes later, Jack and I were outside a quaint Victorian house with teal shutters and a matching sign that read Mattituck Pet Rescue.

"My treat. Since I'm insisting you get a dog, I insist on paying."

"Jack, read my lips. I don't want a dog."

"April, please let's just look." He leaned to my side of the car, put his hand on my thigh, and nuzzled his mouth behind my ear. "I promise, I'll make it worth your while," he whispered, sliding his left hand over my breasts.

"Hmmmm, I'm thinking I should hold out a bit longer."

He slid his hand inside my shirt and cupped one breast, sliding his thumb over my nipple.

"Okay, Jack, you officially have my attention. Oh boy, yep you do." I shifted in my seat and he smiled. "I'll go, but just to look. And I'm holding you to that 'worth your while' thing. Let's get this over with."

Inside the building we found three rows of modified baby cribs complete with dust ruffles. Little dogs had been sorted into the cribs by breed. Bigger dogs pouted in crates on the floor. There were a few people milling about, petting the animals, sticking fingers through cages or watching the dogs play in a central seating area. There was a large glassed-in section with carpeted platforms where a pack of cats preened, lounged, and jumped from one level to another. We passed a crib with four Boston Terrier puppies in it and they started stepping on each other's heads jockeying for position. I reached out to pet one. Suddenly, from nowhere, an older woman appeared at our side.

"My name is Cathy and I'll be glad to help you. I'm one of the foster moms here." She smiled with bright red lips housed under an oversized, fleshy nose. I would swear she was wearing the same green polyester pants Marley had worn last Thursday. I was trying to decide who looked better in them when Cathy continued. "These little guys are just six weeks old. The mom's pregnancy was…" she lowered her voice, "…an accident. We don't want them to know that though." She gave a little laugh. "The mom has since been spayed and the babies are in great health. Bostons are great and fun companions." Cathy lowered her voice again. "Even the illegitimate ones. What kind of dog are you looking for?"

"None. I don't want a dog."

"We're looking for a big scary dog. One that could be considered an attack or guard dog."

"Hmmmm," Cathy said. "Come this way."

We followed her to the back of the house. The dogs there were big. Supersized.

"There are many excellent dogs to choose from. Bouvier de Flanders make great watchdogs and, oh, here's a Great Dane. Her name is Lily. She has a fine temperament and would probably be intimidating." The Dane was a beautiful blue-black and she was uncropped. Her tail alone was a weapon. She licked my hand with her enormous tongue.

"April, she's perfect."

"My house isn't big enough for her, Jack. She's the size of a pony. And again, I don't need a dog. You guys have fun." I wandered off to peek inside cages and cribs while Jack and Cathy moved on to a Rottweiler.

Posted on the outside of each dog "home" was a small, one-paragraph history of why the dogs had ended up at a rescue. Some had been abused, some given up by elderly owners who had gotten sick, and a few needed special care. I found myself making little kissy noises into cribs, fully prepared to hate myself for it later.

One small cage was off to the side in a dark alcove, kind of tucked away off the main traffic route. In it was a tiny Yorkshire Terrier, a ball of long brown and black fur that didn't move even as I came over. I read the synopsis. Despite better my judgment, the Italian mother instinct in me started to take over and the urge to protect and feed was overwhelming. The paper said her name was Loki, she was two years old and her owner had died suddenly. No family or friends stepped in to take her so she had been brought there.

I reached my hand in the cage and gently stroked her. She was soft and silky and very small. She turned her head at my touch and rested it on my hand with her eyes clenched shut. I picked her up and held her to my chest.

"April," I heard Jack call. "Come here. I think we found the perfect dog for you."

I got up, still holding Loki. Cathy and Jack had a Bullmastiff on a leash, ready for inspection. I was prepared to counter the attack with the Yorkie.

"Look, April, this guy is 130 lbs, housetrained and scary." As I looked at the dog, drool escaped his lips, hit the floor and splashed halfway back up again. "This is exactly what you need."

"Oh, are you volunteering to follow him around with a bucket and mop? No thanks. But you will be happy to know that I've picked out a dog."

"Oh, April, that's great. See, I knew you'd find one you'd like. Where is it?"

I nodded to the little fur ball in my arms. "Right here. She's a Yorkshire Terrier and apparently been depressed ever since her owner died. She needs me and her name is Loki." Jack squinted and moved closer to see her.

"Oh, April, c'mon. That's not protection."

"No, April, it's not. That's bait."

"Well, actually, it is protection," interjected Cathy. "Yorkies are fiercely protective of their humans and make very good watchdogs."

"There you go!"

"The problem with this one is that she was well bonded with her owner. Loki's been here for about three months and despondent the whole time. That's why she was off to the side. She's not eating well and doesn't seem to like people coming in all day long poking and prodding. I'm a little surprised she let you pick her up." Cathy went to the desk and rummaged through some papers. "I'm allowed to adopt her out—in fact it may help her,—but you'd have to consent to bring her in once a week for a while so we can make sure she's thriving."

"Ok, that's fine." Pet therapy. Why not?

Jack looked down at the Bullmastiff and sighed. "Can we at least get a studded collar for her?"

"Ugh, April. Joey the Cook is out to get you! How do you think a four-pound domesticated rat is going to protect you?"

I ignored Sal, filled out paperwork and left references while Jack paid the fee, bought food, a pink collar (with teeny tiny studs) and a leash. I promised to bring Loki back for follow-up visits and we left.

We got into the car and Jack said. "I certainly would have felt better if they had priced the dogs by the pound. Do you realize Loki cost about ninety dollars a pound and the Mastiff would have been about three per?"

Loki was still in my arms. She looked toward Jack with huge brown eyes as if she knew he was talking about her.

"Okay, so she is kind of cute," he said. "I'm glad you like her."

"Oh, Jack, I love her. Thank you so much. I think she'll be perfect." I gave him a kiss.

"Well, let's just hope she can bark loud." Jack reached out to pet the dog. She growled and snapped, leaving little indentations on his forefinger. Then she licked my hand, yawned, and went back to sleep in my arms.

"See? I told you she'd make a great guard dog. Now, I think I vaguely remember something being said about you making this adventure 'worth my while?'" I ran my hand down his thigh.

Jack smiled and started the car, "Ah, that, well, first you're going to have to remove the vicious dog from your lap."

"I'm sure it can be arranged."

"Dogs are a great judge of character. Not surprising she wanted to bite him. Hell, there are times I want to." Ugh.

We decided to eat lunch in Greenport. I put Loki's collar around her neck, hooked up her leash and was pleasantly surprised when she walked briskly beside me.

The Hardshell Shack was on the edge of the water, not far from the boat landing. It was the perfect place because it had outdoor seating and we had a dog. We ordered my version of health food—seafood, veggies and legumes: baked clams, fried calamari, and chili fries, served family style. While we waited for it to be served, we watched the small passenger ferry destined for *Shelter Island* pull away from the dock. An obese man sporting a fishermen's hat replete with various hooks stood next to a piling. He had his back to us and was bottom fishing off the edge of the dock. A young couple walking hand-in-hand along the pier walked by, talking to each other and pointing at sailboats. Occasionally I could hear the girl's laughter above the sound of boat engines and passerby.

"April, I need to talk to you."

"April, I was hoping you might be able to help me out," said Jack.

Sal sat in the chair between Jack and me. He was in full scuba regalia, including mask, tanks, and webbed black-and-yellow fins. *"Something's up. I can feel it. Go to the bathroom. Take the dog with you."*

"What's up, Jack?"

"Gillian." He sighed. "She's a girl."

"Ok, you don't get points for being astute my friend, because I'll bet she's been female for most of her life. What's changed?"

"C'mon April. How am I supposed to handle things like her hopping a ferry to see Chris? You're a woman. Did you do things like that when you were younger?"

"April, I have this tingly thing going on down my back. I think we should talk. Something's going to happen."

"Well, Jack, I think it quite possible that you wouldn't want to use me as a reference. I once hitchhiked clear across two states to go meet up with a guy I'd met once at a Grateful Dead concert." Loki started getting a little fussy. I put her down and she started sniffing. I took that as a sign from above, or at the very least from my dead husband. "I think she needs me to walk her," I said, hoping to move far enough away from the table to talk to Sal for a minute.

I moved to stand up. As I did, Loki barked and ran. Unfortunately, when she took off, I was taken by surprise. I barely had a finger on her leash so she went twenty feet before I could take a breath. She headed directly for the pier.

"Loki! Loki! Stop, girl!" I started after her.

The dog ran straight for the spot where the fat man was fishing. He must have heard her coming, because he turned his body toward her. That's when she jumped. Looking something like a hairy flying squirrel, Loki landed squarely on his chest. He lost his balance and, in slow motion, air cycling with his arms, he crashed into the piling, bounced off it, and fell from the dock into the water.

I was still running when I heard a gunshot crack loud enough to deafen me momentarily and feel the air in front of my nose move as a bullet passed only inches from my head.

"DAMN!" I ducked. Since I still had some speed behind me, I managed to propel myself right off the dock into the water, where I landed on top of the fat man. He went under. I remembered reading somewhere that fat cells are lighter than water, so I wasn't surprised when he popped right back up.

"Why don't you ever listen to me?"

"Not now, Sal!" Even though I wasn't far from the ramp, I couldn't touch bottom. I started swimming.

Loki stood looking down from where the man and I had fallen off, her little body perched on the edge of the dock while she barked incessantly into the water.

"Loki!" I heard Jack yell just as I had swum far enough to be able to stand. I could see Jack running, hunkered down. He darted over to the piling and grabbed the dog. Peering over the side, Jack yelled, "April, are you okay?"

Before I could answer, the man Loki attacked stood up in the water, eyes wide and water running from his hair. He looked at me and said, "April? Oh, no! Not THAT April?"

The couple on the dock was close enough to hear our exchange. The guy gave a short, high-pitched shriek, turned around and started back the way he came, briskly. His girlfriend followed him.

Something about the fat guy was familiar. "Are you insane?" he yelled. "Don't you have any control over your dog? My fishing pole is gone, who's going to pay fo…"

He looked at me. Recognition occurred in stereo and we both gasped.

"You!" I said.

"No. You!"

"Uh, oh."

Jack was the last to figure it out. "Damn! April, do you know who this is? It's Earl. From-the-winery Earl."

"Um, April, you just botched up hit number two. The grapevine here says that the bullet was for him! Oh boy, this is bad. You should have gone with the Mastiff...or the llama."

"You're a lot cleaner and a lot less drunk than the last time I saw you. "So let me ask, did you expect to be shot at today?"

"I expect to get shot almost every day, lady. There are some bad people after me."

"Well, it seems they're after me, now, too, and I hear it's all because I saved your ass. Want to tell me why that might be?"

"Nope, just watch it. I think you might want to join a monastery or something for a while."

"Ha! You in a monastery! Funny."

"No funnier than you making it to heaven, Babe." Damn, that one slipped.

Jack, clutching Loki to his chest, walked to the ramp just as Earl and I emerged from the water. Jack asked "April, what the heck was that about?"

"I don't know, but someone out there has a gun and tried to shoot me. Him. Both of us."

Jack shot me a glance and then, focusing on Earl said, "You're in the Fenders, right?"

Earl looked at Jack and shook his head in disbelief. "That's one heck of a stupid question to ask me. Lady, be careful out there. And keep that dog of yours under control. That's one crazy-ass animal. And stay the hell away from me."

"Wait…who is this Joey the Cook guy and why does he want us both dead?"

"Because he's not a nice man. Understand, the less you know, the better off you are, believe me."

"I still think I'm owed some sort of an explanation. Oh, and a 'thank you' might not hurt, either. I mean, I did save you twice."

"April, this is just so weird. Somehow I know that all is not as it seems. Remember I said I thought he was on the 'good' list? I can't shake that feeling. It doesn't make sense that he'd be in with the wrong crowd."

We heard a police siren in the distance. Earl started at the sound, and got visibly agitated as it grew louder.

"This is my cue to get out of here. Look, lady, I can only hope I don't ever see you again." With that, he sloshed away headed for the sidewalk, apparently hoping he could blend his vast dripping bulk in with the summer crowd.

Jack put his arm around me and guided me toward the table.

"April, aw cupcake, you're shivering."

"Cupcake? Where did you get this yahoo from? Cupcake…"

Jack pulled me into his arms and held me tightly, cheek to cheek, kind of rocking me back and forth for a minute. I started calming. I also started warming up nicely but noticed our food had been brought to the table so I shelved the thought of unbuckling his pants until dessert.

I grabbed a piece of fried calamari and popped it in my mouth. The shivering ceased. "That's better," he said.

"More hypoglycemia than hypothermia, I think," I said as I popped another one, dipped in a hellishly hot chipotle sauce this time.

Jack laughed and pulled his chair closer to mine. He grabbed my hand. We began canvassing the area, looking around, belatedly considering that there might be another shot.

"You scared the hell out of me, April. I think you need to consider going out of town for a bit. Maybe I can take you to Connecticut for safekeeping?"

"Really Jack? Which parts of me would be safe then?"

"We don't know if that bullet was for Earl or you. Remember? Joey the Cook? And your car, April, can't forget the car. You need protection and the only way I can think to do it is to get you out of here."

A police car pulled up next to the ramp. An officer stepped out and started talking to the couple who had been on the dock looking at sailboats. The girl turned and pointed at me.

As the policewoman closed the distance between us, Jack reached across the table and put his hand over mine. "It'll be ok. We'll just tell her what we know and maybe we can find you a bulletproof burqa or something."

It was Babbit the Wabbit. She recognized me, too. She shook her head and pulled a seat up to our table.

"April! I feel like I'm in déjà vu hell. I've seen more of you in the last 24 hours than in the last 24 years." She paused for a moment. "So your car has been redesigned, your neighbors reported a fire on your porch this morning, and now people are shooting at you. Anything you want to tell me?"

"Well, I'm not sure they were shooting at me. They might have been after the fat guy. My dog...sort of attacked." I didn't want to pursue this line of discussion or Jack just might whisk me away. Better to sic her on Earl. "Hey, do you want some food?" I waved my hand over the table.

"What food?"

"Huh?" Loki was standing smack dab in the middle of the table, her little legs straddled over what was left of the chili fries. I apparently just failed my first test as a new dog mother.

"Loki!" The dog paused when she heard her name, gave me a passing glance, and turned her attention back to the plate. I picked her up, wondering just how dangerous her back end was going to be with all that chili in her.

We filled the Babbit in on what happened while we ate what little food Loki had left us.

When we were done, Babbit screwed up her nose and said, "Under the circumstances, there isn't all that much we can do. Just be real careful, April, okay?"

"Are you going to tell me to join a monastery too?" I glanced over at Jack, who gave me a stellar smartass smile.

"Well," she said. "As a matter of fact I was going to suggest you go out of state for a bit. A few weeks should do it, until this all calms down. By the way, I thought you'd be interested to know: Elvis Presley is nowhere to be found."

"Huh?"

"They released him?" asked Jack.

"Well, seems he signed some papers requesting discharge. He then disappeared, like someone whisked him away. One minute he was in a hospital bed, the next he was gone. They've searched everywhere, but since he did have the proper papers in order, he isn't a minor, and no one has reported him missing, there isn't much to do. I just thought you'd want to know that he is fine, thanks to you and Marley."

"I'm relieved to hear it."

"I need to go check it out. It kind of sucks that I'm not read into this one. Catch up with you in a bit."

"Ok," said Babbit. "You're going to be careful, yes?"

"Yes."

Jack interjected, "I'll keep her safe. Don't worry. I'm not leaving her side until this is cleared up."

Babbit smiled and winked at me. "Well you have fun with that, guys." She left.

Death Is A Relative Thing

Chapter 13

"Death is terrifying because it is so ordinary. It happens all the time."

— Susan Cheever

We got to the house around five o'clock. The gaping hole in the porch was still there, verifying that I hadn't dreamed all this crap up. There were three notes on the kitchen table. Brian was at the mall, Chris was at the movies, and Scott was with his friends. No one was planning on being home for a few hours yet. I set Loki down to explore the house a bit, put some water in a bowl, and skipped giving her any food until after I was sure the chili wasn't coming back to haunt me.

"Mmmmm, we're all alone." Jack moved behind me, put his arms around my waist and nuzzled at the back of my neck. "You know, I made a promise, and I never renege on a promise."

Death Is A Relative Thing

His hands skimmed the bottom of my shirt, slid underneath and began to move upwards. He found my bra and pushed it up over my breasts. I looked around, afraid I'd see Sal materialize wearing a Playboy bunny outfit and singing the "Itsy Bitsy Penis" song or something similarly obnoxious. I didn't, so, I got back to business. Turning to face Jack, I reached around my back and unclasped the bra. Easy access and all that. He brought his head down to my chest.

I'd removed his belt and was working my way around the waist of his pants. I felt his body. There was a soft layer to him but under it was a well toned abdomen. My mind was racing. How under endowed was he? Was it possible that I wouldn't be able to find it at all or, worse yet, laugh when I did? What if I couldn't figure out what to do with something so small? Could I just claim I forgot how to have sex to save face? My hands were almost to ground zero, about to explore the outer limits and get an answer to these questions when there was the sound of a large vehicle pulling into the driveway. Moments later, a door slammed. We pulled away from each other and I held my breath.

The doorbell rang. We heard little footsteps come running from the living room. Loki stood in the foyer, her stance wide and protective, barking. It was a surprisingly big sound for such a small dog.

"Shit," I said.

"Don't answer it. There's no rule that says you have to, you know."

Three quick raps on the door were followed by "April! April, are you home?"

"Don't answer it, huh? That's my mother and she has keys."

"Shit." He zipped and buttoned his pants, then started fussing with my bra hooks.

It was reminiscent of an incident in 1979 when some scrawny security guard caught me in the back seat of a Nova with my high school boyfriend. I couldn't hook my bra then either. I settled for straightening my shirt over it.

My mother's key was in the lock, turning, when I got to the door.

"Mom! What's the deal?" I was standing in the doorframe.

"What's the deal? April, do you know you have a burned-out crater in the center of your porch and," she leaned her head to the side a bit to get a better look, "a barking rodent in your foyer?"

I said, "Ma...it's my new watch dog. Her name is Loki."

"Watch dog? Oh, April, please. Listen, are you going to let me in, or are you going to wait 'til I fall and become lost forever in the black hole behind me?"

I paused to weigh the options for a second, but then realized she was probably being facetious so I let her in. Loki barked, my mother stared her down. It was over in a matter of seconds. Loki crept away, tail between her legs, looking for something less intimidating to yap at, like maybe a Tyrannosaurus Rex.

We walked into the kitchen where Jack was putting on water for tea. "Oh, Jack. Nice to see you again." My mother picked up the remote and pointed it at the small television on the counter. As it turned on she asked, "So, April, have you seen the local news report?" She pointed the remote again and clicked to the local news station.

"Uh, no." I watched in horror as my face filled the TV screen. "Uh, oh."

The camera pulled away and panned Marley, the kids and my front yard. A news anchor with big teeth, bigger hair, and still bigger breasts was speaking.

"This isn't the first time April Serao has been in the news," the bimbo said. The newspaper photo from *The End* appeared for a few seconds. "In addition to almost killing Elvis Presley, there was a recent incident at *Trefal Wineries* where Ms. Serao allegedly saved a drunken patron from a falling light fixture. Now there has been another chilling incident. It has come to the attention of local Channel 16 news that earlier today police were called in to investigate to a report of gunfire on the docks in Greenport. The responding officer discovered that Ms. Serao was the unknown assassin's target." The anchor's 1,000-watt smiled dimmed to a somber pout. "However, witnesses say that Ms. Serao was not injured, although she did take a leap into the water with an unidentified man whose connection to the shooting remains a mystery at this time."

"Wow, she sounds disappointed that I'm still alive."

"Well, are you PMSing? That could explain it."

"Really, April, when were you going to tell me? That people are shooting at you, I mean? I just wish I could read a paper or turn on the television without finding out that my daughter is the headline." She clicked off the broadcast. "You know there are easier ways to keep me in the loop. Crystal ball, smoke signals or…oh yeah…pick up the phone maybe." She took a breath. "What exactly is going on here?"

Jack said, "Joey the Cook is trying to kill April. But don't worry, I don't plan on leaving her side until this is all sorted out."

"Who is Joey the Cook?"

"Huh? He's not staying here!"

"Of course he's staying here," I said aloud.

"Joey the Cook?" asked my mother, looking around the kitchen.

"I am?" asked Jack, looking at me.

"Of course you are."

"Over my dead body!"

"That one's been taken care of, Sal." Shoot! Did it again. Both my mother and Jack stared at me.

"Uh, oh. The jig's up."

"April, is Sal here now?"

"Yeah, ma, he is."

Jack asked, "Your mother thinks Sal talks to you too?"

My mom turned to face him, "Look Jack, I don't think he talks to her."

Jack looked relieved.

She continued. "I *know* he talks to her." She crossed her arms in front of her body, silently daring him to say anything that would defy her.

Sal appeared, grinning ear to ear and leaned against the counter wearing classic black-and-yellow firefighter bunker gear—the regulation helmet, big black boots, the fifty-pound coat—and holding a heavy duty hose. I heard Loki's little paws hit the ground and she came running. She stopped at my feet, looked directly where Sal was and yapped.

Death Is A Relative Thing

"Look, April, call your friend there Butchie. His mom called him that when he was a little boy. Of course, if she only knew how little her poor boy actually still is…"

I ignored the dig and said, "Jack, Sal says that your mother used to call you Butchie." Another yap from Loki.

Jack stopped mid pour. "Huh? How did you know… Ok, let's just drop it for the time being."

"Guys, I'm just going to run upstairs and get changed, ok?" The harbor may be quaint, but it smells more like canal than Chanel." I took Loki with me.

As I started up the stairs my mother yelled, "Good idea April…you might want to put on a bra that stays hooked, too." Busted. Literally.

I closed the door to my room behind me. Sal was standing at the foot of the bed looking very handsome and firefighter sexy.

"Sal, what's the word?"

"Oh, damn, Babe, your timing—as always!—is horrendous. Remember when Chris was born, right there in the truck? Damned good thing it had a big bench seat. Do we have to do this now? Some of us guys were just going to compare." He held his hose up so I could see. *"I was a shoe-in for the Biggest Nozzle category, if you'd waited just another five minutes…"*

"First of all, my timing was fine, it was your son's that was way off. Too bad, too—I would have liked to have been able to keep those overalls. Second…hose measuring goes on in heaven? You're kidding me, right? There's testosterone up there?"

"Nah, but old habits die hard. You're looking sweet today, by the way." He looked me up and down. *"You aren't going to*

let that Jack attack stay here, are you? It's not like he's much protection."

"Sal, I have the boys here, and I'm worried that something else like what happened to the porch might happen again. Having two sets of adult eyes and ears can't hurt."

"What about me? I have eyes and ears too, you know." Sitting on the edge of the bed, he took off his helmet and scratched at his hair. It was sweaty and matted. He looked at me and my heart hurt.

"Look, Sal, what am I going to do? I miss you so much, but I'm here and you're there...so close and yet..."

"Yeah, Babe, I know. I also know you gotta do what's right for you." He gave me a sad, sideways smile. *"It would be a great time for a hug right now. I wish I could. I'm sorry, April."*

"No, Sal, don't be sorry. It's just that I feel like I have to ask your permission to have a relationship." Loki gave a quick yap.

"Would it help if I said it was okay?"

"It would be better if you said you wouldn't watch!"

"Ok, I won't watch."

"C'mon Sal, what body parts have you got crossed?"

"There's a rule about that, April. Celestial voyeurism is an ethical violation and all sorts of reports have to be filled out if it happens. If I pop in and find you doing something, well, that I shouldn't see, I need to remove myself from the situation, not discuss it with you or anyone else and fill out a 'HALO' report."

"HALO?"

"Yeah, a 'Heavenly Angel Lewdness Override' report. Basically it's like a Get Out of Jail Free card for invading

someone's privacy. I have to let the Inspector General's office know it happened and as long as it doesn't continue to happen, it's ok. But, if it isn't reported and someone finds out later, well, that's a different story."

"What can they do? I mean it's not like you can get fired."

Looking Sal's way, Loki barked.

"True, but who wants to be cleaning the latrines with a toothbrush?"

"Funny, Sal... Listen, I think Loki knows you're here. Do you notice she keeps looking at you and barking?"

"It happens sometimes Animals have a sixth sense and many can hone in on the energy of angels."

"Well then, I guess I have a "Sal radar.""

"Yeah, well, I'm not sure it's worth all the walking and feeding," he said. *"I can just say heya."* He smiled and slowly faded away.

Downstairs, Jack had made up the airbed he'd used the night before. He'd also brought his computer in from the car, and was sitting on the couch trying to log in to his office in Connecticut. My mother had already left, having accomplished her goal of trying to make me feel guilty for being 46 and not checking in with her every time I farted sideways. I looked I started to feel a little hemmed in, surrounded by Jack, Sal, and the yapping fur ball.

I wasn't used to such close monitoring. Was it necessary for Jack to stay here until further notice?

"Hey, Jack, I do appreciate your concern, but you don't have to stay and babysit me. I'm a big girl."

Looking up from the computer, he said, "Yeah, April, I do need to stay. It has nothing to do with you being able to take care of yourself. Someone with no morals and a dangerous streak is after you and your family. That scares me. I can't go back to Connecticut knowing this and doing nothing about it."

He was sweet. Truthfully, I was a little nervous, especially for the boys. I guess it couldn't hurt to have him around. "Ok, I understand."

"Besides," he smiled broadly. "If I'm not mistaken, you need a ride to work tomorrow."

"Oh, damn! I forgot to call the auto body shop. I can't go without my car for very long."

"April, it's Sunday night. No one's going to be there. Call in the morning."

Loki started yapping and I heard the front door open, then close.

"Mom! Where are you?"

"In the den, Scott."

I heard him say, "What the hell?" When he came into the room, his arms were pushed away from his body.

Loki was in his hands, wriggling all around, yapping nonstop as he stared at her like she was going to spontaneously combust or something.

"You're not serious about this are you? This is the guard dog you bought?" Scott asked.

"Yes, and what a fine one she is. She knew you were coming through the door. She barked."

"Yeah, mom, she did. She also macerated your clogs."

Jack smiled broadly as I simultaneously hyperventilated and ran to the front hall to assess the damage.

I heard Sal in the background. *"The clogs, eh? I think this dog has potential."*

Chapter 14

"To get the full value of joy you must have someone to divide it with."

— Mark Twain

After the craziness of the weekend, I was looking forward to being in my cubicle and listening to someone else's problems. It took me almost 40 minutes, but I did get Jack to understand that he didn't have to accompany me to my desk. After I promised three times not to leave the building until he picked me up, he grudgingly dropped me off at TCS.

"Heya Sunshine," said Carl when I entered the lobby. "What's the matter?"

"What makes you think there's a problem?"

He looked at me, his green eyes sparkling and a slow sexy smile playing across his face. I thought, certainly not for the first time, that it was a shame—for me, anyway—that he had a boyfriend. Damn lucky for his boyfriend.

"Well first off, April, you're on time. Second, you're wearing sandals."

"Damned clogs were bigger than the dog, but she ate them anyway."

Carl laughed as he hit the buzzer to let me through the door.

At my desk, the first thing I did was call the number on the business card about my car. A deep voice answered. "Max's Auto Body. What can I do for ya?"

"Hi, my name's April Serao. My car was brought there over the weekend, a red Mini Cooper. Are you Max?"

"Nah, Max is my mother. Hold on a sec and I'll get her."

I heard the phone clank onto a counter, listened to footsteps and some papers being shuffled through. The phone was picked up and a voice identical to the first one spoke.

"This is Max. You're calling about the Mini Cooper, right?"

"Whoa, what kind of game is this? You're Max? I just spoke with you. I thought you went to get your mother."

"I am her mother. Listen, lady, you want to talk about your car or what?"

"Well, yeah. I own the red Mini Cooper that was towed in on Saturday. I need to know how long it will take to fix."

"Well, the damage from the accident isn't too bad—headlight, rear fender and tailgate damage mostly. The car runs and we've worked with your insurance company before so I don't think that part will be a problem."

"Problem? What do you mean by 'that part'?"

"Yeah, well, we had to cut it down from the tree. That'll cost ya. Also it's gonna take some time—depending, lady, on whether you want to leave the graffiti. Would go faster if the car didn't need to be repainted. A lot cheaper too. I'm not sure the insurance company is gonna pay for that since it didn't happen in the accident."

"Well someone needs to pay for it. Since it happened while it was at your shop, how do I know you're not responsible?"

"Hey, I didn't see it come in. I also have a sign posted that says to leave the vehicle at your own risk. For all I know you could've been driving around with it like that for months."

"So you're telling me that my car was hung and painted while on your property, but it's not your responsibility."

"Exactly."

I was ready to yell, but remembered my midlife crisis was in her hands. "How long to fix it?" I figured I'd argue later.

"Two, three weeks with a paint job. Three days if you leave the trendy skull and crossbones."

I choked. "Three weeks without my car?"

"Yeah well, that's about the best I can do. And that is assuming, of course, that I don't have an episode or go off my meds, in which case, it will take longer."

Episode?

"Hang up the phone, April. You don't want to tangle with her. Talk to Babbit. Maybe she can give Max a quick visit and persuade her to do the right thing."

I asked Max to fax me an estimate for the paint job and gave my ok to start the body work.

I hung up the phone, sighed, and leaned back in my seat.

Rob stuck his head around the wall of the cubicle, his hologram-perfect face registering concern. "Seems like you need a little break there, kiddo. How about we go out to lunch later? Marley and I are treating, ok?"

To my credit, I remembered my promise to Jack and momentarily hesitated. I then, however, convinced myself that he couldn't possibly have meant that I shouldn't go out with Rob and Marley. Additionally, I was sure some body part had been crossed when I made the promise, therefore negating it completely.

"Sure, sounds great," I said. I picked up my first call of the day.

At twelve we climbed into Rob's Jeep. "The usual?" he asked.

Marley and I nodded in unison, and he chauffeured us to our favorite lunch hangout, Taco Peña. It was a great little seasonal place featuring outdoor dining, bright umbrellas atop vividly painted wood tables and killer tacos, and the best-kept secret in the area—a little off the beaten path, and thus it wasn't overrun by the Hamptons crowd.

Today it was standing room only, with the line of people waiting for orders coming out the door.

"Hey guys, grab me two chicken burritos and a coke and I'll save us a table before they're all taken," I said.

"Good idea, April," said Rob.

Approximately 25 tables were placed around the small building. Since it was 85 degrees and sunny, the side near the door, which had the most shade, was pretty packed.

I worked my way across the front toward the left side of the building and I found a table near the back that was empty and looked fairly clean. As I closed in on it, I felt someone grab my wrist. I turned and found myself face-to-face with Earl.

"What the hell! Earl, what do you do, follow me?"

"You're kidding right? Listen, lady, I'd be thrilled if I never saw you again."

"Let go of me! And what do you mean by that? I'm a pretty nice person, you know." I struggled to wrench my hand free.

"April, stop. You and I have to talk." He didn't loosen his grip.

"I have nothing to say to you."

He looked me straight in the eyes. "Yeah, but I've got a lot to say to you. Listen, I'm not who you think I am. Sit down—we don't have much time, and I can't let you get into the middle of this again. Your timing sucks."

"I've heard that before."

We sat and Earl slowly released his grip on my arm.

"Hear me out. I'm not part of the Fenders. I'm a special vice agent in squad 26 out of Suffolk, and I've been working undercover for months trying to infiltrate the gang and get some useful information to convict this Joey the Cook. A few weeks ago I did just that, and now the state has an ironclad case against this guy."

"Oh jeez, April, that's why I keep thinking he's really ok."

"Sal, you're going to tell me that you couldn't get the back story on this thing?"

"Huh?" said Earl.

"Nothing, sorry."

Earl continued, "These guys are thugs, dangerous ones. They're not your usual teenage gang members. They're older and savvy and they're into things like money laundering and drugs. Originally, I was accepted as a 'friend of a friend' and was able to get information, but I turned some evidence over to the authorities proving they were going to 'up the game.' They aborted an attempted mob-style hit because of it. Now the game's over and they're trying to take me out because they know I'm going to testify. Meanwhile, I'm trying to get Joey the Cook into custody because without him, I've got nothing."

"Why didn't you tell me?"

"April, the incident at the winery was my first clue they'd caught on. I wasn't sure at the time that the gig was up and I was still trying to protect my cover. I must say however, that landing on you turned out to be the unexpected high point of that day." He smiled, and I found I was less grossed out now than when he had been the bad guy.

"So what do I do now?"

"Stop getting in the way. Apparently this guy isn't going to think twice about catching you in the crossfire—as evidenced by what happened at the dock. You need to leave. These guys are meeting me here in a few minutes. Rumor has it that Joey is joining us, and I need to manage to keep my ass alive. That leaves me no time to worry about yours," he took a little peek around to my bottom and continued, "as pleasant as that thought might be."

Sal appeared to Earl's left wearing an outfit would have made Sherlock Holmes proud. He clenched a large curved Meerschaum pipe between his teeth, and wore a grey tweed overcoat and deerstalker cap. *The magnifying glass he held to one eye enlarged it to an obscene degree and he looked marginally demented. "Yeah, April, the guy has a point. You should leave."*

Rob and Marley, each carrying a tray, came up behind Earl.

"April, there you are. I can't believe how crowded this place is today. We sharing with him?" Without waiting for an answer, Rob set down the food he was carrying and started sorting the order out.

Doing the same, Marley eyed Earl. "You look familiar. I know I've seen you before."

"No, I'm quite sure we haven't met." Earl looked at me. Sal looked at me. I looked at my burritos.

Rob sat down. "Hey, April, there was an old woman on line ahead of us. She asked if I would give you this." He looked straight at me and gave me the finger. "I asked for her name so you could send her an acknowledgement letter, but all she said is that you'd know who it came from." He began to unwrap his food.

Marley stared at Earl, her mouth and eyes wide open. Her tweezers were nowhere in sight. I kicked her leg and she startled, thankfully snapping her jaw shut in the process, then batted her eyes and fussed for a moment with her hair. I'd never seen Marley in "attract" mode, and I was certain the $4.50 that was just spent on my burritos would be chum if it continued.

Earl looked at me expectantly.

"Guys, maybe we should take this stuff back to the office. It's sooo crowded, and I think I remember promising Jack that I wouldn't leave."

"What are you, crazy?" Marley said without a hiccup in her Earl ogle.

"Nah, let's just eat," said Rob, "We're already here and a few more minutes won't matter any. Look, I promise to take you straight back, ok?" He took a bite of his taco.

Earl shook his head in resignation and got up. "I've been here too long already. Watch yourself, April." He completely ignored Marley and walked toward the tables closer to the street.

Marley plunked her bottom onto the bench with a sigh. "Who was he?"

I opened my burrito and took a bite before answering. "Earl. From the winery. The person I had that candid picture taken with. The guy you thought was gross."

Rob and Marley did their surround-sound impersonation and said "Ohhhhh, Earl."

"Well," Marley said, "The photographer obviously didn't get his good side…"

Sal was trying to light the pipe. *"April, I hate to be a killjoy,"* he lit a match and started sucking on the pipe stem, *"but you do have to leave. Earl's 'friends' are going to see you here. Maybe Joey himself is lurking somewhere. Babe, you gotta go."*

"Ok, Ok, I get it. Guys, I have to take care of something. Just meet me at the truck when you're done." I re-wrapped the burrito in a bag and stuffed it in my purse.

Walking towards the outer edge of the seating area, I looked around for Earl. I thought he had moved toward the center of the tables, near the front. I kind of wanted to see the people that were threatening my family. Then again, maybe not. They were scary.

They hung my car from a tree and violated it with two different colors of spray paint. They burned a hole in my porch and shot at me. I wanted to see them, yeah, but they were downright dangerous, and I didn't want them to see *me*.

I spotted Earl five or six tables away. Two young men walked toward him, one dressed all in black—T-shirt, jeans and boots—the other dress wearing all in white—long-sleeve dress shirt, casually rolled up at the sleeves and unbuttoned through the chest, white pleated chinos, white dress shoes, and a light grey vest. Polar opposites.

Sal appeared next to me.

"Stay put. I'll check the situation out, but I want you nowhere near them, got it April?" He waited for me to nod, left and went to their table.

Normally an order barked out like that would force me to do exactly the opposite just on principle, but I was inclined to agree that I should stay away. I did have a problem, though. I could see pretty them well, but I couldn't hear them, so the way I figure it, I had to scout for a better venue.

The two guys sat with Earl and I could see them all talking calmly enough. Sal sidled up next to the guy in black and pulled out his magnifying glass. Holding it in front of him, he peered through it, inspecting him from his shoes to his head. When Sal had finished with thug number one, he moved to thug number two, stepping over them and, to my surprise and mild disgust, even walking through them to get the best vantage point. He pulled out a pad and took a few notes while he sucked at his pipe, which had perversely refused to light. Sal came back over to me.

Death Is A Relative Thing

"I need to get back there, April, but I did find out a few things you should know. First, Earl is in a lot of trouble. These guys have guns, big ones, and they've given him an ultimatum. Either he goes with them quietly, or they will start shooting randomly at the lunch crowd."

Huh? "Oh, not good Sal, what do we do? That's insane. We have to warn them!" I started to hyperventilate, which pushed me into a panic attack. "Sal, I can't breathe."

"Pull yourself together and calm down, April. Cup your hands or find something to blow into."

I remembered the burrito. I pulled it out of the bag, stuffed the burrito into my purse, and breathed into the bag. My brain started to clear. Picking beans out of my checkbook for a month seemed a small price to pay for restored sanity.

"April, it's ok. Earl's agreed to go with them quietly in exchange for keeping the patrons safe. My guess is the reason they made this their venue is that they wanted to be able to make a stand—you know, give him an ultimatum he couldn't refuse."

"Ok, so what else did you find out?"

He took a breath and continued, *"The guy all in black is Junior. I don't know a lot but what I do know is pretty gross. He has a severe case of halitosis and a marked dandruff problem, making black shirts a poor wardrobe choice. The guy in white is Joey the Cook himself. He's got a powdery substance all over his clothing. I doubt, with the kind of quantity he's wearing, that it's cocaine. It's probably confectioner's sugar or flour, but I wasn't about to give him a taste test."*

"So what do we do?"

"I'm going to trail Earl. I want to make sure he stays safe. You are going to go back to the office and stay there. I'll get back to you when I know more."

We watched as the three of them stood up. Sal positioned himself between Junior and Joey. In the distance I heard a dog yapping. Impossible as it seemed, it sounded like Loki. The noise was getting closer and it didn't take more than a few seconds before I realized it *was* my dog. I spotted her running from the parking lot, and watched as she stopped, looked around, and then bee-lined for the table Earl was about to leave. She hunkered her little body down into a fighting stance right in front of Sal and proceeded to yap incessantly.

Sal looked down at Loki and shook his head. I saw him mouth the word, *"Bait."*

A voice trailed behind her. "Loki!" It was Jack. Great. Now there was no way I could tell him I'd never left the office. Since I was already over my head in hot water and up shit's creek, I decided to change seats. I couldn't hear anything from where I was and it was driving me crazy.

I spotted a couple leaving a table, so I crossed the yard and seated myself two tables away. Luckily, it was at the corner of the building, giving me some coverage. I could hear everything. To see, all I had to do to see was move my chair out a bit and peer around the building.

"Loki! Loki, damn it, what do you think you're doing?" The leash was in Jack's hand, and her tiny studded collar was attached to the end of it. As he approached the table, he noticed Earl. "You! Again!"

"Jack, this would be a perfect time to take your dog and leave."

Loki, solidly planted, barked on. I knew she was yapping at a ghost, but to anyone else, it probably looked like she was fixated on Earl.

"Yeah, I'm not exactly thrilled about seeing you again either, but I'm looking for April. Have you seen her?"

Joey the Cook looked surprised and started panning the crowd looking for me. I pushed my chair back to the wall. I couldn't see him any longer, but more importantly, he couldn't see me. I heard him say "April? She's here?"

"Oh, great! Ya know, April, your boyfriend isn't too slick."

Meanwhile, I saw Marley snaking around the maze of tables. She cut in front of me, but didn't notice me. I took a chance and peeked around the corner in time to see that although I was still undiscovered, Earl had not been not so lucky. Marley saw him, broke out in a broad smile, and performed a "come hither" bobble-head hair toss that was terrifying even from a distance. I repositioned myself back against the wall and yelped when I saw Rob sitting across from me.

"Damn good trick. How did you get here?"

"Marley and I saw you skulking. It was obvious who you were avoiding so we decided to divide and conquer. What the heck is going on?"

"I don't think I have time to explain," I said.

"Try. The condensed version."

"Ok, the upshot is that Earl is a cop, and he's after the Joey the Cook, the guy dressed like the Pillsbury Dough boy over there.

Don't know why he's named that but it is a little scary thinking this guy may have prepared me a meal at some point. I really want to find out where he works.... Anyway, in addition to wanting Earl dead, Joey's also after me, as I seem to be guilty of accidentally saving Earl every time Joey tries to kill him. His cohort is a nasty dude named Junior. Neither is a particularly good person and one of them has horrendous dandruff and bad breath. They've threatened Earl and he's going to leave with them so no one here gets hurt. Meanwhile, Jack came looking for me, which is trouble since I told him I'd stay at the office today but I had hidden body parts crossed when I promised. He recognized Earl, asked about me, and now the goons are pretty sure I'm here."

"Ummmm, which hidden body parts?"

Sigh.

"And how did you cross them? Ok, never mind. This is what we're going to do. I'm going to put you into the Jeep and get you out of here before you get hurt."

"No, Rob. I can't live looking over my shoulder all the time. Jack is here. My dog is here. I can't leave them. Besides, these guys screwed big time with my Mini."

"So what are you going to do?"

"I think it's time I introduced myself." Before I could grow a brain and talk myself out of it, I stood up and traversed the distance between the two tables. Earl saw me, grimaced, and smacked his head. Sal groaned, Jack glared, and Marley scowled, supremely pissed that I interrupted her flirt fest. The dastardly duo smiled broadly. They had their backs to the parking lot. I placed myself across from them, sandwiched between Earl on my left and my dead husband to my right who—probably on purpose—had left very little room for Jack on the other side of him. Rob stood behind me.

The study in white said, "Oh, lady, you are a pain in the ass."

"I don't know how you can say that when we haven't even been introduced. You don't know anything about me, so I'd like to start all over again with you guys."

I put on my most convincing "I truly do give a shit" smile, stuck out my hand, and said, "Hi, I'm April. April Serao."

It took a few moments but it registered first with Junior. He blanched, scooted two steps back and said, "April Serao? The lady who....oh, no! You're THAT April?"

The ramifications of shaking my hand quickly dawned on his partner. He withdrew and also took a few steps back. They were both in a sudden hurry to leave.

They backed up, and in doing so ran right into Officers Babbitt and Jeffries.

Junior and Joey tried to backpedal and retreat the way they came but Earl had moved into position behind them. Babbit snapped a set of handcuffs on Joey the Cook, saying, "Oh, you have no idea how bad this is. I get real cranky when I miss a meal, especially during PMS week."

"Yeah, and I have a low blood sugar thing going. I'm already feeling mean," said Jeffries. They led Junior and Joey the Cook to the squad car.

Earl laughed. "Oh yeah, those guys will be well taken care of, don't you worry." He got into his own car and followed the officers as they left the parking lot.

Jack folded me into his arms and kissed me. Quietly he said, "I was so worried. I'm so glad to see you're ok, I'm not even going to yell. At least not now." I scooped up Loki and Jack drove me back to work.

School was out so we decided to spend the following day with the kids. Jack stayed another night and picked Gillian up from the ferry. Afterward, he cooked, and my boys eagerly ate their way through their second breakfast in as many days. I was outside on my hands and knees fishing the newspaper out of the hole in the porch and cursing the delivery guy when Sal popped in.

"Hey, listen, Babe, I need to talk to you. Nice ass, by the way."

Sal was sitting on the porch railing, dressed in the clothes I liked to think of him wearing: leather jacket, Freedom Ride T-shirt, jeans, biker boots

He had startled me. "Sal! What's up?"

"The big guy ordered my halo. It should be finished in about five business days."

"Oh. Sal, I'm glad for you."

"Well, Babe, I appreciate all your help. We always did make a good team, April."

That was true. We always were good together. "No problem Sal, I've had a lot of fun. But what happens now? Do you have to leave? Am I going to ever see you again?"

"April, honey, the rules state that under normal circumstances angels aren't allowed to hang out with the living. On top of that, you do have a boyfriend...." Sal positioned himself in front of me so closely that I could swear I smelled his Brut cologne. He looked me right in the eye. *"And for exactly that reason I've asked*

St. Peter to allow me visitation. I mean, April, if truth be told, you need someone to watch out for you."

"Oh, really!"

"Babe, just look at the yahoo you picked. You need all the help you can get. I think you qualify for an Assigned Angel, first class."

"And you would be that angel, eh? So, what was St. Peter's verdict? Yes or no?"

Sal laughed, blew me a kiss, did a little finger wave and disappeared.

I had just plucked the paper from the abyss and stood up when I heard the truck pull in. My mother exited the Suburban, her heels clicking as she marched down the driveway and then navigating the danger zone that was my porch. Without hesitating, she nodded in acknowledgement, opened the front door, and let herself in. I followed. Loki ran down the stairs fully prepared to yap, noticed it was my mother and quietly retreated to the laundry room.

"So, April," she began, while walking to the kitchen, "guess who I ran into?" She noticed the boys and Gillian at the table eating breakfast, gave them a perfunctory nod also and turned to me.

Jack was cooking at the stove. "Marie, would you like a Belgian waffle?"

"No, thanks. I want April to guess who I ran into."

"Who, Ma?"

"Guess."

"Ma!"

"Mrs. Mitzner. Remember her?"

186

Oh boy. "Yeah, Ma, I do. How is she?"

"Well, she had a close call. She went to the doctor and they found a blockage near her heart that could have been fatal had she waited much longer. Fortunately it's easily correctable now. I thought you might have known about it."

"Why would you think that?"

"She wanted me to thank you for the heads up. In fact, she was so grateful she wanted you to have a small present as a token of her appreciation."

My mother opened her purse and handed me a gift bag.

I reached inside the bag and my fingers touched something smooth and rubbery. My throat began to swell and I started sneezing. Latex!

I heard Sal laughing. *"This shit just never gets old."*

Death Is A Relative Thing

Epilogue

It was after midnight. I clicked off the television in the den. Jack and Gillian had gone home. As nice as it was to have had the company, and as much as I liked Jack, I was glad to have my house to myself again. I wasn't sure where the relationship was going to wind up, but Jack still wanted to see me, voices in my head and all, so it was going as far as Connecticut, at least for the weekend. I was planning to take the ferry over to visit him. I wondered if there were any restrictions concerning angels and interstate travel.

Loki sat at my feet and I tripped over her when I stood. That's when I realized how abnormally quiet she'd been. I sat back down and for some time listened, undisturbed. I eventually came to the same conclusion Loki had: Sal was gone.   ,

Sleep didn't come easily. As difficult as it had been to coexist with a ghost, I'd gotten used to having him around, and I felt oddly comforted knowing he was there for me and the boys. Now though, he was lost to me all over again. The empty place, the pain way down deep inside me that over the years I'd learned to coexist with, was wrenched open. I cried hard and long.

I held his ring tightly in my palm as I slept. My dreams were fragmented, bits and pieces of reality, slices of understanding surrounded by pure nonsense. I walked past the Pearly Gates, which had been newly decorated with colorful painted flowers, and saw Mr. Mitzner, wearing a satin vest and a visor at a crowded casino-style table dealing blackjack. He looked up and waved at me. Booming out of a nearby loudspeaker was Elvis singing his new hit song, "Wet, Wet Willy."

A white wood podium appeared in front of me and an angel with enormous wings that shimmered like mother of pearl hit it with his gavel. The orange-yellow glow cast by his halo surrounded both of us. It could only be St. Peter. Staring directly at me, he said in a thundering voice, "April, I have deliberated the request before me that you have an angel assigned to you full time. I have read the reports and weighed the possible repercussions and I have reached a decision, which is…"

At that moment, church bells started going off in my brain— loud, incessant. I watched St. Peter and although his lips moved, I couldn't hear the verdict because of the bells. The ringing started changing timbre, becoming less of a vibrating sonorous church bell sound and more of a whiny electronic BEEP BEEP BEEP. My alarm clock. St. Peter faded away without my ever having heard the verdict.

I bolted out of bed, late again, and jumped into the shower. I couldn't be sure, but I could have sworn that while I was washing my hair someone said, "Hey, Babe. Nice ass. But you better haul it to work." Loki cocked her head, and I knew that one way or another, I'd be okay.

Death Is A Relative Thing

CPSIA information can be obtained at www.ICGtesting.com
Printed in the USA
LVOW091648231011

251661LV00004B/7/P

9 781934 606087